MASSACRE AT BLUFF POINT

Ethan Craig has only just started working for Sam Pringle's outfit when Ansel Stark's bandits bushwhack the men at Bluff Point. Ethan's new colleagues are gunned down in cold blood and he vows revenge. But Ethan's manhunt never gets underway — Sheriff Henry Fisher arrests him and he's accused of being a member of the very gang he'd sworn to track down! With nobody believing his innocence and a ruthless bandit to catch, can Ethan ever hope to succeed?

Books by I. J Parnham
in the Linford Western Library:

THE OUTLAWED DEPUTY
THE LAST RIDER FROM HELL
BAD DAY IN DIRTWOOD
DEVINE'S LAW
YATES'S DILEMMA
DEAD BY SUNDOWN
CALHOUN'S BOUNTY
CALLOWAY'S CROSSING
BAD MOON OVER DEVIL'S RIDGE

I. J. PARNHAM

MASSACRE AT BLUFF POINT

Complete and Unabridged

LINFORD
Leicester

First published in Great Britain in 2007 by
Robert Hale Limited
London

First Linford Edition
published 2008
by arrangement with
Robert Hale Limited
London

British Library CIP Data

Parnham, I. J.
  Massacre at Bluff Point.—Large print ed.—
Linford western library
  1. Western stories
  2. Large type books
  I. Title
  823.9′2 [F]

  ISBN 978–1–84782–396–0

Published by
F. A. Thorpe (Publishing)
Anstey, Leicestershire

Set by Words & Graphics Ltd.
Anstey, Leicestershire
Printed and bound in Great Britain by
T. J. International Ltd., Padstow, Cornwall

This book is printed on acid-free paper

1

'You looking for work, cowboy?'

Ethan Craig leaned forward in the saddle, nodding as he considered the approaching rider.

'Sure am,' he said. 'You reckon there's any on offer?'

'Don't know. I'm doing the same as you are — looking for work.'

Ethan exchanged names with his fellow would-be cowpuncher, discovering he was Jeff Tyler. Around them the milling herd of longhorns rumbled back and forth, the distant cries of the drovers urging them on so they could complete their mission. Twenty yards ahead was the chuck wagon where the owner of the outfit Sam Pringle was completing the handing over of his latest charges to a local rancher. Ethan had already caught Sam's eye and they'd traded smiles.

1

Now he was waiting for the chance to persuade his old friend to take him on.

While he waited, he chatted with Jeff, learning that he had come from the nearby town of Bitter Creek where he'd become tired of working as a teller at the bank and had decided to try cowpunching instead.

'Bank teller,' Ethan mused, 'now that sure sounds one hell of a lot less exhausting than this life. Maybe I'll give that a try if there's nothing available here.'

'It didn't interest me,' Jeff said amiably while peering around, 'but then again the grass is always greener elsewhere. You got any idea who we need to impress?'

'Sam Pringle, and he's a good man and a good friend.' Ethan noted the flash of disappointment that clouded Jeff's eyes. 'But don't worry. I'll put in a good word for you.'

Presently Sam concluded his business and made his way over to Ethan, a huge smile breaking out.

'Ethan Craig,' he declared. 'I ain't seen you for a while. You looking for work?'

'Sure,' Ethan said. 'I heard you might be a few men short for your next drive.'

'Then you heard right. Two men left a month ago and I've been struggling. I'm heading over Prudence way to start up again in a few days, so if you two are minded to join up . . . '

Ethan had been down to his last few dollars but he reckoned his fortunes were about to change and he whooped with delight, while Jeff provided a more subdued grunt of pleasure. So with a quick shaking of hands the two men joined Sam Pringle's outfit. By now the ranch hands had taken official possession of the cattle and so Sam led them over to meet their new colleagues, who were all in high spirits. Everyone was ready to head off to spend their money on several nights of well-earned entertainment. Their only problem was where they'd go.

'I ain't heading to Bitter Creek,' Rory Scott, a red-headed and seemingly permanently smiling man, said. 'I wasted a night there with Isaac a few days ago and I can tell you, it sure was the deadest place I've ever set foot in.'

Jeff shuffled from foot to foot and muttered something under his breath. Only Ethan noted his discomfort.

'I reckon,' Miles Osborn said, slapping a thigh with a mischievous grin spreading across his face, 'when we ride into town we'll sure liven 'em up.'

'I don't know,' Rory persisted as several men hooted their support. 'Like I said, I've been to livelier funerals than that night in Bitter Creek.'

The men cast uncertain glances at each other as they waited for one of them to make the decision as to where they would go. Jeff spoke up first.

'Speaking as someone who's lived all his life in Bitter Creek,' he said, pausing to look at Rory, letting him suffer a moment of embarrassment after his previous comments, 'I have to disagree with you. Bitter Creek sure is a mighty fine town.'

'No offence meant,' Rory murmured, looking shame-faced.

'None taken. It may be mighty fine . . . but it sure is as dead a place as I've ever seen.' Jeff smiled while everyone grunted a laugh. 'But luckily I know somewhere livelier — Fall Creek. It's further away and it's not so grand, but the liquor's cheaper, the women are prettier, and the town's a whole lot rowdier all round.'

'Yee-haw!' Rory shouted, Jeff's declaration effectively deciding the matter without further debate.

'I reckon you're just the man our outfit's been looking for,' Miles said, slapping Jeff on the back as they headed to their horses.

Jeff took the lead in directing everyone off on what he said would be a two-hour journey. Ethan took the opportunity to ride alongside Sam Pringle and they exchanged tales of what they'd done since they'd last seen each other. They chatted amiably while around them the other men bristled with excitement about the forthcoming chance to unwind.

After riding along for an hour that excitement was growing, but Ethan noted that after his initial animated enthusiasm in directing them towards Fall Creek, Jeff remained quiet. He also noted something about his behaviour that sent a tremor of concern rippling through his guts.

He didn't want to alarm the others and so he hurried his horse on to ride alongside him. They were now riding across the plains with an enormous bluff a quarter-mile to their side, rising upwards like a giant, angry pimple, gleaming red under the rays of the lowering sun.

'What's wrong?' Ethan asked, keeping his voice light and untroubled.

'About what?' Jeff replied quickly.

'You keep on looking around, and mainly at that bluff.'

'It's called Bluff Point and it's

probably nothing.' Jeff shrugged. 'But I reckon I saw something flash over there a few minutes ago.'

Ethan glanced to the side at the bluff without moving his head.

'Flash as in somebody signalling?'

'That's what I thought. I first saw movement a few miles back, as if someone was following us. Now I reckon that person's holed up on the bluff.'

Ethan considered Jeff for a moment. 'I ain't the kind of man to judge another man. I'm sure you've got your reasons for wanting to leave town. You can tell me what those reasons are, or you can choose not to. It doesn't matter to me. But if you reckon somebody has a problem with you, now might be the right time to tell me about it.'

Jeff shook his head, his light smile putting Ethan's mind at rest.

'Nobody is after me.' He nodded back, signifying their trailing companions. 'But the same can't be said about the others. Eight men all just been paid might interest the kind of people who've been around recently.'

'Any people in particular?'

'The bandit Ansel Stark has got a lot of people worried.'

'Never heard of him, but no matter, we should slow down and talk to Sam.'

Jeff sighed. 'Do you get the feeling we picked the wrong day to join this outfit?'

Ethan snorted a low laugh, but then shook his head.

'I prefer to think we picked the right day. Maybe we can make a difference.'

Jeff supported Ethan's positive thinking with a grunt. Neither man did anything untoward to draw attention to himself and Ethan ensured he rode alongside Sam Pringle to pass on the information.

'Rory, Isaac,' Sam said after considering Ethan's news, 'you headed into Bitter Creek recently. Did you get yourself into any kind of trouble?'

'No!' both men blustered with apparent indignation although their darting eyes suggested they'd overstated their conviction. Several men uttered snorts of laughter, suggesting there probably had been an incident, but one they hadn't mentioned to the outfit leader.

Sam sighed, considering them. 'Could well be that somebody like this Ansel Stark is spoiling for a fight, but nobody is taking our money off us, no matter what . . . ' Sam trailed off then looked at Ethan. 'Did you see that?'

'Sure,' Ethan said. The flash of light had been unmistakable, coming from high up on the bluff.

Open plains were to their left, suggesting that avoiding the bluff would be their safest option, but Sam still asked for opinions. Most agreed with this plan, but after some thought Sam provided his decision, uttering his words using the kind of quiet authority that Ethan remembered and which always ended a discussion immediately.

'I reckon if someone is up on the bluff signalling, then he's signalling to someone out there, and they're the people we need to avoid. We should head to the bluff and find somewhere to make a stand.'

Everybody glanced at each other, nodding. Only Jeff responded.

'We're about ten miles out of Fall Creek,' he said, 'but I know of a pass that takes you through Bluff Point. It's winding and treacherous so not many people use it, but it'll cut miles off the journey, and might mean we don't have to make that stand.'

After that pronouncement everyone looked at Sam. This time he didn't reply for a full minute, his jaw rocking from side to side as he considered the options.

'All right,' he said at last. 'Everyone bunch up, then on Jeff's call hightail it to the bluff like the Devil himself is on your tail and don't look back for nothing.'

Grim grunts sounded from the men. Then they rode on quietly, waiting for the call. Jeff played his part well by gradually pulling away from the group and veering slightly towards the bluff. Ethan kept his gaze on what appeared to be a solid wall of rock, but clearly Jeff knew what he was looking for because he suddenly raised a hand, then yanked his horse to the side and surged away.

Everyone hurried after him and in a straggling line they galloped for the bluff. Ethan fell in towards the back to ride beside Sam and, despite his orders, Sam did glance back over his shoulder. Ethan caught his momentary flaring of the eyes and this encouraged him to also look back.

Barely more than 300 yards behind them six men were in pursuit, having appeared seemingly from nowhere. When he turned back, for the first time he saw the gap Jeff was taking them through, opening up between two towering blocks of stone.

Jeff slowed as he rode into the gap, but as soon as he emerged into the rising, boulder-strewn and winding pass he tugged back on the reins, making his horse rear as he struggled for control.

'Trap!' he yelled as several gunshots rang out. 'It's a trap!'

The group bunched, their horses spooked and bustling into each other as their riders struggled to identify where the shooting was coming from. A volley of gunshots thundered around them, some whistling over their heads, others kicking up pebbles from the hard ground. Ethan saw a man to his right clutch his shoulder before the force of the blast tipped him from his mount.

Behind them the pursuing men were closing, trapping them between the two groups.

'Get to cover!' Sam shouted.

Nobody needed any further encouragement to leap down from their mounts and run to the sides of the pass, seeking out the best cover available. But now their attackers had them in their sights.

Miles got a bullet in the back. He ran on for a few paces before he dropped to his knees then bit the dirt. Isaac went spinning round to land on his back as lead tore into his side. A second shot ripped into his supine form and ensured he would never get up again.

Ethan gained the cover of a pile of boulders first and knelt, then shouted encouragement to the rest to follow him to relative safety. He slapped Jeff, then Rory, then Sam on the shoulders as they passed him. Nobody else followed them.

'Is this all we're getting?' he shouted, venturing a glance beyond his cover. He got his answer when he saw the bodies. Everyone else had perished in the initial onslaught.

'Five years to get together the best damn outfit in the state,' Sam said, anger darkening his face, 'and these varmints wipe them out for a few dollars.'

'Save your anger for later,' Ethan said. 'We have to find a way to fight back before we join 'em.'

As Sam glanced out into the pass, then darted back when a bullet scythed over his head, Jeff shuffled round to sit with his back to the pass. He looked up to higher ground, his eyes glazed and staring, perhaps with shock or perhaps as he took stock of the lie of the land. Behind them Rory bobbed up to trade gunfire with their attackers but immediately a sustained burst of gunfire whistled around him and he dropped back down.

'Reckon as we need to spread out,' Rory said.

'You're right,' Sam said. He pointed at Jeff and Ethan. 'You two head up there and see what you can do.'

Ethan slapped Sam's shoulder as he left and with the shocked Jeff trailing behind him they scurried from covering boulder to covering boulder, gaining some height. When Ethan paused for breath and looked down, what he saw sent a shiver down his spine.

A dozen men were scurrying around at the bottom of the pass. They were aiming to launch an assault on Rory and Sam, and if these were just the men they could see, Ethan didn't like to think how outnumbered they were.

'That sure is a lot of men to take on one small outfit,' Jeff murmured unhappily.

'Yeah,' Ethan said, 'against that many Sam and Rory don't stand a chance, no matter what we do. We have to get them up here.'

Jeff nodded and grabbed a handful of pebbles to throw down and attract Sam's attention, but already he was too late. The attackers swarmed across the pass in a wave of gun-toting mayhem.

Two men must have already sneaked up on the outfit's position because they suddenly appeared on either side of Sam and Rory. Sam was quick enough to take one of the men out, but not to get the other and Ethan's guts churned as he saw his old friend get a bullet in the stomach that kicked him backwards into a boulder.

Rory fared just as badly, getting cut down by the same man. Ethan aimed, then loosed off a round of lead, but from over 100 yards away he failed to hit anyone. Worse, a solid block of men surged over the boulders and fired off round after round into the two wounded men, ensuring they'd never fight back.

With all the attackers having grouped so close together Ethan reckoned he couldn't fail to hit some of them. He aimed at the centre of the group, but before he could fire, Jeff slammed a hand on his arm and dragged him down to the ground.

'What you doing?' Ethan grunted.

'Saving your life,' Jeff said, his wide and dead eyes displaying a mixture of fright and hopelessness.

'I can see you're right worried, but we ain't getting out of this alive unless we start fighting.'

'Facing that many men I don't reckon we've got any chance, other than one . . . perhaps they won't realize we're up here.'

'That's a slim hope!' Ethan blustered.

'It's the only one we've got,' Jeff said,

his voice growing in strength and displaying increasing conviction. 'Think. If the raiders planned this then they would have watched the outfit. They wouldn't be expecting there to be ten men here. Unless they had eagle eyes and were paying real close attention, they might not even realize we'd joined them.'

'But they must have seen us come . . .' Ethan trailed off, sighing as Jeff provided a forlorn smile that acknowledged it was a long shot, and so, reluctantly, Ethan had to admit he was right.

Keeping their heads down and hiding was the only chance they had of avoiding becoming the final victims of this massacre at Bluff Point.

2

Five minutes after the last gunshot echo had faded away Ethan let himself hope that Jeff's long shot of staying hidden might just pay off. When another five minutes had passed and the raiders still hadn't found them, Ethan started to relax, but it took a full half-hour before he accepted that the plan had in fact worked.

Down below the raiders were milling around and from their occasional shouted comments to each other Ethan gathered they were dragging the bodies into the open. Each man was then searched and thrown over the back of a horse. Then they made ready to move on, taking all the horses with them. He didn't hear anyone talk about searching for more members of the outfit.

With Ethan now believing they'd survive, a more important thought

18

began to concern him — the need to observe everything the raiders did in the hope that one day what he saw might help to bring them to justice. He edged up from behind his cover to look down into the pass, but from around 100 yards away he couldn't discern the features of the men below. Their clothes weren't distinctive and although he screwed up his eyes he saw nothing that would help him identify these men later.

'Be careful,' Jeff urged from beside him, his shaking voice still betraying the shock he felt.

'I am,' Ethan said, 'but I have to watch them.'

'I know, but maybe they'll leave some clues behind, and besides, there's a good chance that that is the notorious Ansel Stark and his bandits.'

Cheered by this thought Ethan shuffled down until just his eyes peered out from between his two covering rocks. He watched the raiders ride off, seeing them move out from the shadowed interior of the pass and then leave his view. He looked at each person, hoping that something about one of them would prove to be noteworthy, and he was rewarded for his vigilance when the last man left the pass.

This man stopped and looked back at the scene of the massacre. His roving gaze appeared to pass over Ethan's position, then drift back to look towards him. Although it was unlikely that he would be able to see him, Ethan had the distinct impression that they locked gazes, and as if in response to Ethan's harsh glare, the man removed his hat and mopped his brow.

Ethan was treated to a vision of the man's bright-ginger crop of hair shining in the low sunlight, appearing for a moment almost as though the hair were aflame. Then the man replaced his hat, turned his horse, and was gone.

Two hours later Ethan and Jeff traipsed into Bitter Creek, footsore and weary. Jeff's suggestion that maybe the men would leave some clues as to their identities hadn't proved to be correct and so they had put their faith in getting to town as quickly as possible and alerting the law. Although the outfit's original destination was Fall Creek, Jeff reckoned they were more likely to get help in the larger town.

As it was, Sheriff Henry Fisher considered the terrible news without so much as a flicker in his stern gaze.

'A massacre at Bluff Point,' he said with a resigned sigh when Ethan had finished relating their tale, 'again.'

'Again?' Ethan said.

'Pretty much the same thing happened to the Clancy family. That damn Ansel Stark must still be out there, except he's now moved on to picking off innocent passers-by.'

Ethan nodded, looking around the sheriff's office as he gathered his thoughts.

'Would this Ansel have ginger hair?'

'No,' Fisher said, giving Jeff a quick glance for the first time.

'Ethan saw a man with ginger hair amongst the group,' Jeff said, to which Fisher replied with a shrug.

'Hopefully,' Ethan said, 'this fresh trail will help you track him down.'

'Not much hope of that. Ansel's a devious critter and that's a fact. This long after the massacre I doubt there'll be anything useful to find, and he's careful enough not to leave a trail.'

Ethan stood silent and aghast, with his heart beating with an insistent rhythm for several seconds before he found his voice.

'You mean you're not doing nothing about it?'

'Didn't say that,' Fisher snapped, waggling a reproachful finger at Ethan, 'and you don't tell me how to do my job. I just ain't wasting my time heading out to Bluff Point again.'

With that statement of intent, Sheriff Fisher turned his back on Ethan and Jeff, leaving them to look at each other, shrug, then take the only option available of leaving the sheriff's office.

'Can you believe his attitude?' Ethan said, stomping to a halt on the boardwalk.

'Doesn't surprise me,' Jeff said. 'After the Clancy family died Fisher led a posse that searched every inch of the hills, but they didn't find anything. I reckon he has his reasons for not going after Ansel.'

'So you knew about the Clancy family,' Ethan mused.

'I did. What you getting at?'

'I find it odd that despite what happened to them you still led us past Bluff Point.'

Jeff flashed a pained glance at Ethan, then removed his hat to thrust his fingers through his hair in a nervous and perhaps irritated gesture.

'It never occurred to me that Ansel would strike twice in the same place, and to be honest I'm doing my best to forget about what happened to the Clancy family.' Jeff gulped and replaced his hat. When he spoke again his voice was sad and it croaked several times as if he was fighting to pick the right words while trying not to think about what he was saying too much. 'I was the one who found their bodies and it was because of what I saw that day that I decided to leave town. I just had to get away. I just . . . '

Jeff sniffed and lowered his head. Although Ethan found this explanation odd Jeff was clearly distressed, and besides he now had more pressing matters on his mind.

'I guess that must have been a terrible thing to find,' he said, 'but now I've lost everything I owned to that Ansel Stark, so do you reckon you can get me a horse?'

'Yeah, sure . . . ' Jeff raised his head, his eyes narrowing. 'You heading back to the bluff?'

'Sure am. If the law ain't interested in finding Ansel, I'll have to do it myself.'

'It'll be dark in an hour. This ain't the right time to do this.'

'There'll never be a more right time.'

Jeff sighed. 'Then I guess I'd better come with you.'

Ethan shook his head. 'Sam Pringle was my friend. I have to go. I don't need no help for what I have to do.'

'I wasn't aiming to help. I'm coming to try to talk sense into you.'

The sun had set and darkness was gathering when they arrived back at the bluff and although their search of the pass again failed to find anything that Ansel's group had left behind, they had no trouble finding their tracks. Ethan began grumbling that this was contrary to the care that Sheriff Fisher had claimed Ansel Stark showed, but then fell silent when Jeff quickly deduced where Ansel had headed.

'He must have gone towards the Clancy house,' he reported.

Ethan nodded. 'Then that just saves me a journey.'

While they rode out of the pass Ethan decided that despite Jeff's reticence about talking, he had to know what had happened to the family.

Jeff took several deep breaths before he spoke and when he did his eyes were glazed and distant in the poor light.

'It sure was terrible. Three days ago I went out to discuss Eugene Clancy's loan, but I found him and his family shot to pieces. Five sons and their parents all gone in a single day.' Jeff shivered. 'Nobody found either of the two daughters.'

'Perhaps that's why Fisher wasn't too interested, then. Two women who might still be alive are more important than eight dead men.'

Jeff gave a non-committed shrug and a worried frown that said he really didn't want to talk any more about this matter.

The house sat beside the bluff, a spring providing an explanation as to why the Clancy family had settled here. The house itself was intact, but the row of graves set out behind the house suggested that nobody would hurry to take over the homestead, or at least, not while Ansel Stark was still at large.

Curiously, the horse-tracks they had been following stopped beside the graves. When they searched around they even found fresh footprints that showed the gang had dismounted and wandered all around the house and particularly beside the graves.

'Now that sure is odd,' Jeff said.

'Anything you can think of that Ansel might have wanted so badly that he returned?'

'Nope. The gang stole everything they could carry.' Jeff shrugged. 'I guess he must have had his reasons.'

'And I'll be sure to ask him what they were when I catch up with him.'

Contrary to Sheriff Fisher's comments the trail away from the house was also obvious, going broadly westwards, and Ethan moved to his horse, aiming to head off and follow it, but Jeff raised a hand, halting him.

'I don't reckon we should go any further,' he said.

Ethan nodded. 'So this is where you try to talk me out of going after Ansel, is it? Well, say what you have to say, then I'll be going while I still have some light left today.'

'From what I saw in the house and back in the pass, Ansel Stark is a ruthless man. You don't stand a chance of facing him and a whole heap of bandits on your own. Leave this to the law.'

'Anything else?'

'It seems like you've got a trail to follow, but it's sure to lead nowhere, or be a feint, or a trap. Fisher was right. Ansel is careful and devious.'

'Anything else?'

Jeff provided a sigh of exasperation. 'I can think of plenty more reasons. There's the fact that — '

'I'm obliged for the advice,' Ethan snapped, cutting Jeff off, then he offered a smile. 'We ain't known each other for long, but people who know me like Sam Pringle did reckon I'm the most bull-headed man they've ever met. So save your breath, you can't talk me out this.'

'I did have one final thing to say before you talked over me.' Jeff raised his eyebrows. 'Before you go, give me back my horse.'

Ethan was prepared to disagree with anything Jeff said, no matter what the nature of his argument, but this comment brought home the one fact he couldn't ignore. He didn't have a horse of his own, or money, or anything other than the clothes he wore.

Ethan stared at the trail of hoofprints that disappeared into the gloom ahead, then let his gaze rise to the outline of the distant mountains, imagining all the places in which Ansel Stark could have gone to ground. He let his shoulders slump, then sighed.

'I guess I do need to get myself some money before I go after Ansel.'

'You do.' Jeff gave an encouraging smile. 'But look at it this way: Ansel Stark probably hasn't gone far. He's raided near to the bluff twice in the last few days. The odds are that staying in Bitter Creek might just be the best way you'll have of catching him.'

This thought cheered Ethan and so, in a more optimistic frame of mind, he headed to his horse.

'What're you going to do now?' he asked as they set off back to Bitter Creek.

Jeff whistled a resigned breath through his lips.

'That disastrous escapade makes me think I ought to stay in town, after all, and that means I ain't got much of a choice but to go back to working at the bank.'

'Any chance of work there?'

'Now that's sensible talking,' Jeff said. 'I'll put in a word for you with Emerson.'

When they arrived back in town Jeff did more than put in a word for him with the bank manager. It turned out that Ansel Stark's recent activities had made Emerson twitchy, so he'd decided to employ a guard to stand by the door.

Although this wasn't the type of work Ethan would have looked for, he accepted Emerson's offer. Emerson also paid him in advance, enabling him to get a room at the local hotel. He spent the night alone recalling good memories of his old friend in a respectful tribute that kept at bay the murderous thoughts that he knew would occupy his mind come the morn.

When he started work the next day he found that his duties weren't onerous. He quickly settled into the task of merely standing by the door and scowling — following the manager's instructions of making everyone think he'd hired a tough gunslinger — at every customer who came inside.

For his part Jeff resumed working in his old position as a teller. The occasional scowl and bored expression he delivered in Ethan's direction suggested he wasn't enjoying the work. Ethan soon saw the reason for his irritation when he noticed what an argumentative and demanding man the head teller Duggan Ward was.

But seeing this man focused Ethan's

mind on to the grim task that awaited him. Behind his back the other tellers called Duggan by the nickname of Ginger and in accordance with this name, he had a shock of bright-red hair.

In fact Duggan Ward's hair was so striking it appeared to be on fire in the bright sunlight that streamed into the bank — a vision Ethan had last seen when he'd watched the last man leave Bluff Point after the massacre.

★   ★   ★

'It's him I tell you,' Ethan said, pounding a fist on the bar for emphasis. 'Duggan Ward is the man I saw out at Bluff Point.'

Jeff sighed. 'Just because Duggan's hair is the same colour as another man's you saw from over one hundred yards away, it doesn't mean he's a member of Ansel Stark's bandit gang. I've known him for years and I can't say I like him, but that's just not possible.'

It was early evening and Ethan had completed his first day of work at the bank. Jeff had bought him a drink in the town's only saloon. In accordance with Jeff's earlier comments about the town, it was a quiet establishment, but Ethan didn't mind. The peacefulness gave him time to think, and right now he couldn't help but obsess about what felt like the only lead he had on tracking down the men who had murdered his old friend.

'I know what I saw. I only got a clear view of one man and he had bright red hair, the kind you can't help but notice, the kind you don't see that often.'

'Except on Duggan Ward and on this man from Ansel Stark's gang.' Jeff shook his head, sighing. 'Duggan is like me, a bank teller. He might dream of doing something else with his life, but that sure as hell doesn't involve joining a gang of bandits and massacring eight men for a few dollars.'

'Then there had to be a reason why he joined that raid beyond stealing their meagre pickings. From what I know of them, Sam Pringle's outfit was a decent group of men, so I doubt they'd done anything wrong to attract such an attack, but maybe that doesn't go for Duggan. Maybe he got dragged into something he didn't want to do. Maybe — '

'Maybe. Maybe. Maybe! Don't sound to me like you've got many facts there.'

'Except I have one.' Ethan leaned towards Jeff and lowered his voice to emphasize his intrigue. 'I asked around and Duggan wasn't at work yesterday. Now that's mighty odd seeing as how the bank was short-handed after you'd left.'

Jeff couldn't provide a ready answer to that other than to just shake his head.

With Jeff not responding, Ethan let the subject drop, but he had no intention of letting the matter end there. He reckoned he'd have to work at the bank for a month to earn enough to buy himself a horse and have sufficient spare money to embark on what would probably be a lengthy manhunt. He vowed to spend that time learning about Ansel Stark's activities, and he also reckoned that finding out about Duggan Ward's activities wouldn't do any harm either.

Accordingly, when Jeff left him Ethan propped up the bar, spinning out his drink to avoid spending too much money, as he awaited confirmation of the other piece of information he'd uncovered about Duggan. An hour later that piece of information proved to be correct when his quarry entered the bar and ordered a drink, as he did every night.

He chatted with the bartender for ten minutes then left, as he did every evening according to the gossip Ethan had encouraged in the bank today. Ethan waited for a minute, then downed the dregs of his whiskey and followed him out into the darkness.

He stopped just beyond the batwings. Duggan had only walked for a few yards before he'd joined two other men. All three men were walking slowly away from the saloon and none of them looked back at Ethan, but Ethan recognized the other men as being Jeff Tyler and Sheriff Fisher.

Ethan idled against the wall in the shadows to let them get further away. After talking for around thirty seconds the group parted, with the sheriff heading off to the law office and Jeff crossing the road. Duggan Ward stopped to watch both men leave then ambled off down the road.

Ethan followed him, matching Duggan's leisurely pace and ruminating on why the lawman and Jeff might have been speaking to him, especially as Jeff didn't count Duggan as being a friend.

At the end of the road Duggan turned the corner, heading towards the bank. Ethan speeded his pace but even so, when he looked around the corner Duggan was no longer visible. He had been out of his sight for only a few seconds and in that time he shouldn't have been able to find somewhere to sidle into, but clearly he had.

Ethan ran his gaze up and down the shop fronts, seeing that all of them had closed for the night and there were no alleyways. Feeling bemused Ethan set off down the road looking left then right in the hope that one of the many shadows on the road would resolve itself into the form of Duggan Ward. He had made his way past the first two buildings when he heard talking, the low words preceding his noticing two men standing close together in the doorway of a mercantile.

Both men silenced instantly. Although Ethan drew his hat down to prevent them seeing his features in the low light, he was able to note that Duggan was one of the men. He couldn't see the features of the other man. As soon as he'd passed Ethan heard footfalls and the boardwalk creaked, giving him the impression that they'd come out of the doorway to watch him leave.

Ethan kept his gaze on the boardwalk

ahead. Presently he heard shuffling behind him as, he presumed, the men slipped back into the doorway. Still he avoided reacting and instead maintained his steady pacing before walking off the boardwalk and heading into the road.

On the opposite side of the road the shadows were deeper. When he reached the wall of the bank he stopped and, as casually as he could, turned. He couldn't see the men, but he presumed that that would also mean they couldn't see him. So he stood by the wall and waited.

A minute passed before both men emerged from the doorway. Without further conversation they went in separate directions. Duggan walked towards Ethan.

Ethan watched the other man disappear around the corner but could discern nothing that would help him recognize him again later. Then he returned his gaze to Duggan. As he came closer, Ethan noticed that Duggan was clutching a bag to his chest, holding it so close that in Ethan's current suspicious frame mind he reckoned he was hiding it from casual view.

When he reached the bank he stopped and looked directly at the building. Ethan kept still, hoping Duggan wouldn't be able to see him. Duggan spent long moments looking towards the bank. A smile appeared, the white arc of his teeth catching a stray beam of light. He delved into the bag. His hand emerged and he looked down at whatever he'd withdrawn. Then he replaced the object in the bag and turned to continue his walk.

Although Ethan couldn't be sure, during the few seconds in which he'd seen Duggan in profile, he thought he'd caught a glimpse of what Duggan had removed from the bag. It was a wad of bills amounting, by the size of it, to several hundred dollars' worth.

★   ★   ★

'I didn't think you and Duggan Ward were friends,' Ethan remarked when he'd finished work for the day and he was heading out of the bank.

'I'm not,' Jeff said as the two men walked down the boardwalk towards the hotel where Ethan was staying.

'Except I saw you talking to him last night.'

'Ah, and I sure regret doing that now.' Jeff stopped and put on a shamefaced look. 'I thought through what you'd said about Duggan being out of town and I had to admit it was suspicious enough for me to mention it to Sheriff Fisher. We checked on it with Duggan and he had a good reason to not be at the bank, but it wasn't because he was out at Bluff Point.'

'And what was that reason?'

'It's irrelevant and private.' Jeff offered a smile that Ethan didn't return, then lowered his voice to an encouraging and friendly tone. 'Has Duggan given you any reason other than this bizarre coincidence of his hair colour to make you think he might be involved in what happened?'

Ethan considered confiding in Jeff about what he'd seen last night, but decided not to. In truth, he wasn't sure what he'd seen. Duggan had met someone in a quiet locale and that man had appeared to give him money, but there could be plenty of reasons for that and none of them connected to the events at Bluff Point. All day Ethan had devoted less time to considering the customers and more time to glaring across the bank at Duggan, hoping to see him act suspiciously, but he'd done nothing untoward.

'No,' Ethan said, 'I guess I've got no reason to suspect Duggan Ward.'

Having said the words, Ethan considered that perhaps he did need to stop looking for reasons to view this man's actions as being suspicious and keep his mind open to other possibilities.

Later, as he lay on his bed staring at the ceiling, he decided this thought was the right one. So he didn't head down to the saloon to follow Duggan again as he'd originally planned to do. He was still sure something odd was happening here, but he wasn't so sure that Duggan was at the centre of it.

Sheriff Fisher had just not been as interested in the demise of Sam Pringle's outfit as he should have been. That attitude hadn't changed when Ethan had seen him earlier in the evening to ask about the investigation's progress. Neither was anyone else interested in discussing the incident when he attempted to talk to people in the bank.

The massacre of the Clancy family did concern everyone, but curiously the hatred that Ethan felt didn't burn in anyone's eyes at the mention of Ansel Stark. Everyone had also decided that the missing daughters were dead by now, and so a search was futile.

Ethan had encountered frontier-town resilience before, in which people recovered from tragedy quickly, but not this quickly. It was almost as if the massacres had never happened and everyone had moved on. Even the threat of more bandit raids concerned nobody except Emerson Drury.

Ethan overcame his irritation at this attitude the next morning though, when he received his first good news for a while. A rancher had found his horse roaming free about twenty miles from Bluff Point.

Even better, and against all his expectations, both his saddle-bags were intact with his clothing inside along with his small stash of dollars that he'd hidden in a spare pair of boots. This discovery bemused Ethan as it contradicted the reason he thought Ansel Stark had raided the outfit in the first place.

As he headed to the bank with Jeff that morning he outlined his predicament.

'I hate to disappoint anyone, especially after Emerson gave me a job at the bank, but now I'm thinking of moving on.' He watched as Jeff nodded and then grunted as if he'd expected this news. 'And I hope you're not going to waste your time trying to talk me out of it again.'

'I won't, and I'm sure Emerson won't mind either. Not many people were enthused about taking the job when he first suggested posting a guard, but it's been a few days since the last raid and Ansel Stark hasn't showed up. I guess others will be keen to think about taking on the job now.'

'Then I'll decide before the end of the day.' Ethan raised his eyebrows. 'After I've had a word with someone.'

Jeff didn't need to ask who that someone would be, and he offered to let Duggan know. Later that morning Ethan saw Jeff talk quietly with Duggan. Both men glanced at him, but afterwards Duggan made no move to come out from behind his desk. As Ethan's instructions were to stay by the door, he had no choice but to wait until Duggan came to him.

The day wore on and, as Ethan paid constant attention to Duggan's whereabouts, he got the distinct impression he was avoiding looking at him. This observation added to his belief in Duggan's guilt and made his decision as to whether he'd leave today that much the harder.

The bank was an hour from closing when the first opportunity to talk to him came his way. Two rough-clad men had just come into the bank and were loitering by the window. Ethan was eyeing them up for possible trouble when Duggan came out from behind his desk to escort an old woman to the door. He didn't usually do this sort of thing, so Ethan tried to catch his eye as he stood to one side and opened the door. Duggan ignored him, but after the old woman had left he took his time in returning to his desk.

'You heard I wanted to speak to you?' Ethan asked.

'I did,' Duggan said in a reluctant tone, not meeting Ethan's gaze.

'You ain't got any more customers waiting, so we could have that word now.'

'I guess we could.' Duggan turned to him and with an unconscious gesture he raised his hat to brush fingers through his red hair. 'Speak your mind.'

'It's like this, I thought I saw you out at Bluff Point when Sam Pringle's outfit got shot up. I might have been wrong, as the man I saw was some distance away, but either way I've taken to watching you. A few nights back I saw you acting suspiciously when a man gave you money.'

This last revelation made Duggan flinch. Ethan judged that he'd expected him to mention the first half of his suspicion, but not the second.

'I ain't got to explain myself to you.'

'You don't, but I'm asking you to do it for the sake of everyone who died out at Bluff Point. The only reason I might stay in town is because of you. If I don't have a reason to stay, I'll head off after Ansel Stark. So what's it to be? Have me tailing you day in day out, or just tell me what you were up to?'

46

Duggan rocked his head from side. Sweat broke out on his forehead and he darted his gaze nervously around the bank. That gaze took in the two rough-clad men who'd come into the bank a few minutes earlier. From the corner of his eye Ethan saw one of the men nod and a moment later Duggan gave a slight inclination of the head.

'What the — ?' Ethan stopped speaking when he saw Duggan spin round and drop to his knees. The other two men matched his action, all three men turning so they faced the door and away from the back of the bank.

Behind the desks their movement caught Jeff's attention as well as that of the other teller, Barney Johnson. Both men looked at the three men who were now kneeling in a hunched posture, bemusement furrowing their brows. Barney came out from his desk while Jeff shot Ethan a concerned glance.

Ethan didn't respond as he could now hear a rumbling sound, then people shouting nearby. He decided the shouting was coming from outside and, as he could see nobody through the window, perhaps from the back of the bank.

Then he received the answer as to what was happening in the most violent way possible. A solid force that felt like an iron fist punched him in the chest, lifted him bodily off the ground, then slammed him into the wall behind him. He saw Jeff clatter to the floor and Barney hurtle towards him, also to smash into the wall, then slide down it to land sitting and stunned. A ringing filled his ears and his vision became clouded, the explanation for this came when he began coughing and realized the bank was full of swirling dust.

He tried to stand but his jarred limbs refused to obey him and he merely rolled round to lie on his side. His hearing returned when he heard someone shout for help, and through the swirling dust a jagged burst of lightness came to him from the back of the bank. At first he couldn't tell what he was seeing but gradually he realized that most of the back wall of the bank was no longer there.

'Dynamite,' Ethan murmured.

'You got it,' a voice grunted in his ear.

Ethan turned to find that one of the newcomers to the bank was leaning over him, his gun drawn and aimed at Ethan's head.

'Who are you?' Ethan murmured, still disorientated.

'You don't ask the questions.' The man dragged Ethan to his feet. 'But Ansel Stark will be asking you plenty.'

3

'Open the safe or die!' Ansel Stark demanded.

Ethan Craig and Barney Johnson shot a quick glance at each other. Both men winced, but neither man moved towards the safe.

It was now an hour after the bank raid and Ethan and Barney had been taken to a house. Although Ethan had been blindfolded on the journey, he was sure from his limited view of the terrain through the window that the house was the Clancy family home, the scene of the first massacre at Bluff Point.

The bandits' carefully planned assault in which they'd come in through the back of the bank had enabled them to not waste time trying to open the safe. Instead they'd secured it with grappling hooks, ripped it bodily from its mooring, and dragged it out of town.

But the careful planning that had gone into the raid had not been perfect. Although they'd taken Barney hostage, a man who could open the safe, Ethan was sure to disappoint them. He had no idea how to get into it and so far Barney had shown no inclination towards co-operating either. Instead, he cast an imploring glance at Ethan combined with a barely perceptible shake of the head.

'Just let us go,' Ethan said, drawing Ansel's attention to him. 'We ain't doing nothing you say.'

Ansel Stark narrowed his eyes. In the flesh he was pretty much as the wanted poster had depicted him, cold-eyed, eager to smile as if he enjoyed his cruel acts. What the picture couldn't convey was his authority. Everyone jumped to his orders without question and the shortness of those commands suggested it would never occur to him that anyone would disobey him.

Accordingly, with a mere wave of the hand he gestured for two of his men to

51

take a firm grip of Ethan's arms and secure him. Then he pushed Barney towards the safe and standing side-on to him, drew his gun and sighted his head.

'Quit wasting time,' he roared. 'Open it, now!'

Barney's former resilience collapsed in an instant and he fell to his knees before the safe.

'I can't,' he whimpered. 'I just can't.'

Ethan struggled, finding that the men who were holding him had firm grips of his arms.

'Leave him alone,' he said, looking at Ansel. 'You want to threaten anyone, threaten me.'

'Obliged for the offer,' Ansel said. Then with an almost casual gesture he pulled the trigger, the force of his gunshot rocking Barney's head back before he flew backwards into the safe and slid down it to lie lifeless on the floor. Then he swung the gun round to aim it at Ethan. 'Now you will open the safe.'

Ethan could only look on with horror as Barney twitched then stilled.

'You didn't have to do that,' he murmured.

'I didn't. He just needed to get me the money, then he'd have lived.' Ansel grinned, his wide arc of yellow teeth and blank, cold eyes leaving Ethan in no doubt that he wouldn't have provided that mercy.

'Why not just dynamite it?' Ethan asked, playing for time as he couldn't see any other option open to him.

'Open it,' Ansel demanded, 'or I will use your idea of blasting it open. Except I'll tie you to the safe and stuff the dynamite down your throat.'

'Then I guess I'll just have to open it.' Ethan waited until Ansel jerked his gun to the side, pointing him towards the safe, then continued. 'But it'll take some time.'

'Take all the time you reckon you need to avoid a bullet in the back.'

Ethan took that comment as meaning he'd bought himself a few minutes, but he was unsure what he could do in that time. To prolong his period of respite he didn't move towards the safe and let the men holding him drag him towards it, then throw him at it.

Ethan lay sprawled over the safe, then pushed himself away from it and rolled his shoulders. He looked with distaste at Barney's body lying hunched on the floor until two bandits dragged it away. Then he stood back and rocked his head from side to side, trying to appear as if he were appraising the safe. Instead, he was looking around the house, judging what his best chance would be of escaping.

Ideally he would have liked to have got some measure of revenge against the man who had shot up Sam Pringle's outfit, but he had no doubt he wouldn't live for long enough to succeed if he attempted that. His revenge would have to wait for a time of his choosing when his own chances of survival were better.

The house had a door, which was behind him, but the nearest window was five paces ahead of him, and it was open and low enough to vault through. As he didn't reckon his chances of getting a gun off one of the bandits were high, he decided his only chance was to wait for a moment when nobody was looking his way. Then he would run for the window and slip outside.

He'd counted ten bandits and they were all in the house, but not all of them were watching him. If he got lucky he would then need to reach one of the bandits' horses before someone came out and shot him. Then he would have to rely on his memory of the terrain and the bandits' unwillingness to leave the safe to make good his escape. It wasn't a good chance, but it was the best he could think of.

'Do it!' Ansel urged from behind, dragging Ethan's thoughts back to his more immediate problem.

Ethan nodded and crouched over beside the safe. He'd be more comfortable if he were to kneel but in that position it would take longer for him to get to his feet and make a run for the window.

He considered the lock and the thought came to him that he had seen Emerson change the combination several times. Although Ethan had been some distance away whenever he'd done it, he closed his eyes, forcing an image into his mind of Emerson turning the lock. Then he put a hand to the lock and slowly turned it in the direction he'd seen him turn it.

He couldn't help but wonder again why the gang had taken him, probably the employee with the least idea about opening the safe, but he fought that thought away. He stopped turning the dial then turned it back. His memory told him the safe required four movements to open it. Yesterday that had been left, right, left, further left, but there were fifty numbers and for him to happen across those numbers would require an extreme piece of luck.

He completed the four motions and forlornly yanked the door. It didn't move. He set the dial back to zero, as Emerson did whenever he made a mistake and had to start again, then moved the dial left, right, left, further left. He tugged.

Again the door didn't open.

Sweat broke out on his brow and his back itched as the feeling overcame him that Ansel would shoot him now as he must have realized he didn't know how to open the safe.

He risked glancing over his shoulder and was greeted by the welcome sight of all the bandits looking through the window by the door. None of them was looking his way. Ethan couldn't believe his luck and he started to move towards the window behind the safe, but his chance disappeared almost as soon as it had arrived. A bandit turned and hurried to the window, barging past him to reach it and look outside.

'They're coming from this side too,' he reported.

'It's Sheriff Fisher,' another man said from the doorway. He ventured a glance outside then darted back in. 'And he's got himself a posse.'

'How did he find us?' Ansel demanded. 'I told you to throw the pursuit off our trail.'

'We did, but he must have figured out where we were going. I said this was a bad place to hole up after what happened here last week.'

Ansel cut off the debate with a firm glare, then barked instructions to his men to take up defensive positions. He swirled round to face Ethan.

'We're leaving in one minute,' he said. 'Either we take the money with us and leave you to make friends with the lawman, or we take the safe and leave your dead body for him to bury. What's it to be?'

Ethan turned back to the safe, said a silent prayer that he'd get himself some luck, then jerked the dial back and forth, appearing as if he were looking for the right combination. But he knew that the attempt was doomed to fail and after giving it one more try, he decided to take the only option available.

There was only one bandit on this side of the house. He had his back to Ethan as he looked out of the window. Two others were checking that the hooks still secured the safe so that they could drag it off. The others were mingling around the doorway, waiting for the posse to come within firing range.

Ethan waited until the two bandits backed away. Then he made his move. He stood back from the safe, rubbed his chin to appear, in case anyone was looking at him, as if he were considering the problem of opening the safe. Outside he heard Fisher shout out a demand. The bandits within responded with a volley of lead.

Ethan reckoned that was his moment to act. He jumped to the side then ran at the bandit by the window.

He got to within two paces of him before the bandit flinched, but with the battle for control of the house raging around him nobody else reacted. He had aimed to knock the bandit over, then leap through the window, but the man turned, his gun swinging round to aim at him. He was too slow. Ethan slammed into him and made a grab for his gun. His hand closed on the bandit's wrist, then walked along it until he got a controlling grip on the weapon. Then he pushed the gun down.

The bandit wasted a bullet into the floor. Then the two men wrestled over the gun, twisting it to the left then the right. People shouted behind him. Any chance of him making his getaway undetected had now gone.

Their mutual grip around the gun squeezed another bullet out, this time holing the roof. Then the bandit took strength from the fact that others had seen them fighting and he grinned at Ethan, who heard footfalls advancing on him from behind.

'Give up,' a voice demanded.

Reckoning that he had but moments to effect his escape, Ethan swung himself round to place his back to the window. The move let him see that two bandits had advanced on him and were awaiting their chance to move in and take him. The rest were trading gunfire with the posse outside.

Ethan gathered his strength and shoved his assailant away. This man tumbled into the other two men, sending them both reeling to the floor.

Then Ethan turned on his heel and bounded to the window. He slapped a hand on the sill, aiming to vault over it. A slug ploughed into the adobe a fraction of an inch from his fingers. Ethan knew the time it'd take him to vault over the sill would be long enough to let the men behind him aim carefully. So to give himself the maximum chance of surviving for a few more moments, as he pushed himself off the floor he did a double-take and ducked and rolled to the side.

He enjoyed a joyous moment when he saw the ground outside the house below him and the hope hit him that maybe he might be able to run to safety. But then an explosion of pain sliced across his scalp and in an instant all strength fled from his body. His limbs collapsed beneath him and he slumped down to lie with his head dangling downwards outside the building.

Wetness ran over his forehead. He saw, with detached bemusement, gleaming red orbs drip then patter down into the dirt almost as if they were emerging from someone else's body. He felt no more pain, but he was aware of himself slithering backwards and could do nothing to stop himself falling. He hit the floor inside the building and lay crumpled. Feet scuffled around him. Then scraping sounded, which he presumed came from the bandits moving the safe.

'How are we supposed to get in it now?' someone asked.

'We've got plenty of time to figure that out when we've seen off the lawman,' Ansel said. 'Now just get it out of here.'

'Where we meeting up?' someone asked, the sound of his voice now faint.

'Black Pass, the usual place.'

Ansel continued to shout instructions to his men for them to move out of the building. Ethan wondered why nobody was paying him any attention. The answer came to him with a slowness he recognized as being proof of his plight.

He was dying. Perhaps he was dead already and was now existing in a purgatory before whatever came beyond.

The voices were echoing. The sporadic gunfire sounded as if it were miles away. Although he couldn't remember closing his eyes, his vision had darkened. He was numb, feeling only a discomfort to his forehead which his mind told him should be painful.

The bandits moved away. He heard shouting as distant echoing cries, then the faint pops of gunfire, then silence. The silence continued for what felt like an eternity. Even in Ethan's serene state he worried that maybe death would turn out to be an endless darkness filled with interminable silence and numbness.

Then he heard someone speak nearby, the words unintelligible, but this change in circumstance brought him no joy.

Someone moved closer and when he heard voices again he understood what the people were saying. There were two men, with Sheriff Fisher identifying the other as being Deputy Sheckley.

'He killed the hostages,' Sheckley said.

'I'd expect that,' Fisher said. He moved over to Ethan who was relieved and surprised when he felt a hand slap down on his shoulder and turn him over to lie on his back. 'Wait! This one is still alive.'

'You sure?' Footfalls hurriedly approached him and despite the blackness Ethan had the impression that two people then stood over him. 'He looks shot to hell.'

Fingers pressed down on his forehead. Then light stabbed into Ethan's eyes as the sheriff prised open his eyelids. Ethan couldn't focus his eyes, instead seeing a blurred shape above him, but with a supreme effort he forced his jaw to move.

'Am I . . . ? Am I . . . ?' he croaked.

'You'll live, if that's what you're trying to ask,' the deputy said. 'You just got a scrape across your head.'

'Lucky . . . lucky,' Ethan said with relief.

'Sure was,' Fisher said, then pushed the deputy aside and hoisted Ethan up to a sitting position. Metal flashed as he turned a gun on him. 'And it was all bad luck because you are now under arrest.'

4

Doctor Price dropped the bloodied towel into the bowl of reddened water then wrapped a fresh bandage around Ethan's head and declared him fit and whole.

The bullet had only broken skin, ploughing a furrow across his scalp without cracking bone. Ethan's vision was no longer blurred, but he still felt groggy; he had the kind of headache not even a bottle of the roughest whiskey could give him, and whenever he made any sudden movement he felt nausea rising. But no matter, he had enjoyed a stroke of pure luck where the difference between life and death had been a matter of a hair's breadth.

His luck had ended there. For some reason Sheriff Fisher didn't believe him to have been an innocent party in the bank raid. So the lawman had insisted that the doctor tend to Ethan in a cell in a corner of the sheriff's office. As soon as Price reported that he'd finished, Fisher ushered him out, then slammed and locked the cell door behind him.

Ethan looked at the sheriff through the bars and offered a smile.

'I'm guessing Ansel Stark got away from you, then,' he observed.

'Yeah,' Fisher said. 'Now, you're the only member of his gang I've got to take to court, but the judge will make you pay on behalf of all of them.'

'When are you going to let me explain myself? I only came to Bitter Creek because Ansel Stark shot up Sam Pringle's outfit. I was all set to go after him, but he happened across me first and took me hostage.'

'That is a good story, but that's all it is.'

'Look at me.' Ethan pointed at his head. 'They shot up Barney Johnson and did the same to me. It's down to a stroke of pure luck I'm still alive.'

Fisher considered Ethan, his sceptical eyes appraising the bandages.

'Some might say you were too lucky,' he said, sneering. 'Some might say you got the sort of scratch a man might give someone to make it look like he was trying to kill that person and so put a lawman off the scent.'

Ethan sighed, searching for the right words to explain himself that Fisher couldn't twist.

'Just because I failed to guard the bank against an armed gang of ten bandits it doesn't mean I was in cahoots with them.' He offered another smile that Fisher didn't return.

'It's too big a coincidence you happened to get that job a few days before the biggest bank raid we've ever had.'

Ethan took deep breaths to calm himself and forced himself to stop arguing with a lawman who was clearly determined to avoid listening to sense. In a soft and reasonable tone he offered the one point he was sure Fisher couldn't argue with.

'You've got a right to be suspicious,' he said, 'but suspicions are all you've got. You need proof.'

'I do, don't I?'

Sheriff Fisher smiled, his unconcerned reaction suggesting he thought he already had enough evidence to prove Ethan's guilt. For the first time Ethan felt a twinge of worry that maybe he wouldn't be able to talk himself out of this predicament.

'What you reckon you got on me?'

Fisher licked his lips, clearly pleased to have provoked a reaction.

'I'll save my talk for your day in court. You can save your talk for the rats, the only ones who're likely to listen to your lies.'

With that statement of contempt, Fisher turned away, leaving Ethan to sit back on his cot and start worrying about just what evidence the sheriff thought he had on him. But no matter how much he picked over the events of the bank raid, and then over his few days of employment at the bank, Ethan couldn't surmise what it might be.

A brooding day passed before Ethan received his first visitor. Jeff Tyler came to the cell and looked at him through the bars. He gave an apologetic smile.

'You need anything?' he asked.

'Other than to get out of here, I guess not.' Ethan stood closer to the bars and lowered his voice to ensure Sheriff Fisher couldn't hear him. 'Why does Fisher reckon I'm guilty? It must be obvious I only stopped off in town because I had no choice.'

'I don't know.' Jeff leaned on the bars and sighed. 'But he's mighty convinced you were involved in planning the raid.'

Ethan kicked the base of the bars, shrugging. He tried to see the situation from the lawman's viewpoint, but he couldn't see beyond the simple prejudice that often overtook common sense whenever there was trouble and a stranger in town was unfortunate enough to be nearby.

'The Clancy family's demise would

have hit everyone hard and I guess it's only natural he's looking for someone to blame, but he has to see that I had nothing to do with the people who killed them.'

'You'd better hope he will, because — '

'That's long enough,' Fisher snapped. 'Leave the prisoner alone now.'

Jeff spoke quickly before he had to leave.

'I've done the only thing I reckon I can do for you. I've hired you an attorney. He should be able to sort this mess out.'

Ethan thanked him, then sat back on his cot.

For the next few days he put his faith in this attorney being able to see through the ridiculous nature of the charges against him and talk some sense into the situation. But when the lawyer arrived he didn't fill him with confidence.

Finlay Smallpiece, of Smallpiece, Smallpiece, & Smithson, was a bored and morose weasel of a man who spent his time with Ethan complaining about his long journey from Prudence. When he did deign to listen to Ethan's story he kept a sneer on his face that suggested he didn't believe a word he was hearing.

Ethan still related his tale, from the moment he had looked for work with Sam Pringle's outfit to Fisher throwing him in a cell. Finlay then warmed to the task and quizzed him on a number of points to clarify the details. Only when Ethan described the terrible moments after the bandit had shot him and he had thought he was dying did he remember a potentially useful piece of information that he hadn't recalled before.

It wouldn't help to prove his innocence, but it was something only an innocent man would reveal, and with Fisher twisting all the facts to put him in the worst possible light, it was perhaps his only chance of freedom. He paused in his tale for effect before drawing Finlay in closer.

'While I was lying there with my head feeling like it'd cracked open,' he said, 'I overheard the gang talking. Someone mentioned where they'd hole up next to open the safe. It sounded like it was their usual bolt-hole.'

Finlay's eyes lit up with interest for the first time.

'You willing to volunteer that information?' he asked.

'Sure.' Ethan cast a significant glance at the cell door. 'But only from the other side of those bars.'

Finlay nodded. 'I get your meaning. I'll fetch the sheriff.'

Unfortunately, when Fisher came over his sneer suggested he hadn't taken the news about Ethan remembering valuable information as a sign of good faith on Ethan's part.

'So you want to bargain, do you?' he said, sneering. 'The first time I saw you I knew you were the kind of man who'd sell out his own kind.'

'That ain't the way it is,' Ethan said. 'I overheard them talking.'

73

'And you've only just remembered this?' Fisher said with heavy sarcasm.

'I have.'

'And you'll only divulge that information when I've let you go?'

'If you're going to play it tough with me, I'll have to do the same.'

'And that's something only a guilty man would do. An innocent man would tell me what he knew and not negotiate for justice.'

Finlay drew Ethan aside and whispered to him that he should still tell Sheriff Fisher everything he knew. Ethan was tempted to comply but he reckoned that Fisher would deem anything he did as being another sign of his guilt. Right now he wanted the comfort of holding on to what was probably his only advantage.

Ethan shook his head, and so the sheriff snorted with derision.

'I just knew you were a member of Ansel Stark's gang. You gave him the signal to start the raid.' Fisher turned away. 'And I can't help but wonder what else you did with him before that.'

'Wait!' Ethan shouted. Fisher swirled round to face him, but Ethan didn't continue speaking. Fisher's claim that he had given Ansel the cue to start the raid had helped him recall another incident from the bank raid that he'd forgotten in all the ensuing chaos. This time he was sure it would prove to be significant when he could put all the facts together.

'Go on,' Fisher snapped.

'I'm not a member of Ansel Stark's gang, but I know for sure that someone else is — Duggan Ward.'

Fisher blew out his cheeks in exasperation.

'So you're still spreading that lie. Duggan had an alibi and — '

'I don't care about his alibi on the day of the massacre. I'm talking about what he did afterwards. Duggan never normally came out from behind his desk, but he did just before the raid when two gang members came into the bank.' Ethan knew he was babbling and maybe later he'd work it all out, but he had to get Fisher's attention while his attorney was here. He paced back and forth while talking, fighting down a sudden feeling of nausea from his rapid pace. 'I thought he'd come to talk to me, but he just distracted me. Then he nodded to one of the bandits. That must have been an order to take me with them because I knew about his activities. And — '

'That's enough,' Fisher said. 'I don't want to hear any more lies.'

Ethan turned to Finlay, hoping his attorney would speak up for him, but instead he shook his head and directed him to sit.

'It'd be better for you if we concentrated on proving your innocence rather than someone else's guilt,' he said. 'Trust me on this.'

And so ended his first and, as it subsequently turned out, only meeting with his attorney.

For the next week he waited for his trial to begin with a grim mixture of anticipation and foreboding. His steadily healing head wound helped to raise his spirits somewhat and with the nausea and headaches receding, he hoped that his one piece of bargaining power would help him.

But any hope he had of receiving justice disappeared within seconds of his entering the courtroom.

Townsfolk packed the room. Everyone was relishing the theatre of the trial by baying for his blood, waving their arms and shaking their fists in a show of universal loathing. Everyone he looked at scowled or swore at him, confirming they'd already decided he was guilty. The nearest he saw to a friendly face was his lawyer, and he just looked bored.

Deputy Sheckley was the first to present his testimony. He covered Ethan's failure to co-operate and the fact he was the only hostage to survive. This led on to the doctor's testimony, which emphasized the luck Ethan had had in not being killed. Apparently, the doctor had never before seen anyone shot from such close range who had survived.

Then various bank customers testified about Ethan's arrogant behaviour and suspicious actions. Nobody had trusted him and nobody was surprised to learn he was a bandit.

Even when Emerson Drury testified he failed to mention that Ethan had glared at each customer because those were his orders, and instead reckoned that it was evidence of his surly nature.

Finlay Smallpiece passed up his opportunity to question the witnesses, accepting their stories with a nod and the occasional whispered comment to Ethan to trust him.

Ethan accepted his wisdom and besides, the constant litany of carefully worded stories, which had quickly begun to sound rehearsed, had lulled him into a forlorn torpor from which he couldn't raise the enthusiasm to complain. Then suddenly he livened up when, against the run of abuse and slanderous comments, someone spoke up for him.

As expected that man was Jeff Tyler. He had been called upon to explain why, in the prosecutor's words, he'd encouraged the manager to employ such a disreputable and arrogant bandit in the bank.

'Ethan didn't want the work,' Jeff said. 'He was all set to leave town, but I talked him into staying.'

'Oh?' the prosecutor murmured, then scratched his head in confusion as he glanced at his notes, which probably hadn't covered this eventuality.

'Yeah,' Jeff said while the prosecutor floundered. 'Ethan was determined to head off after Ansel Stark because he'd killed his friend Sam Pringle, but as he had no money, I persuaded him to work here for a few weeks until he could move on. And — '

'No more questions,' the prosecutor blurted out, getting his wits about him at last.

'But I'm trying to tell you why Ethan

couldn't have been working for Ansel Stark. If he had he'd have — '

'I said,' the prosecutor insisted, 'you can step down.'

Jeff continued talking, but the prosecutor pointed to the door and the judge banged his gavel to still the audience's growing disquiet, which was drowning out Jeff's words, so he flashed Ethan an apologetic smile and shrug, then left.

While the next witness headed to the dock, Ethan leaned towards Finlay.

'You need to call Jeff to speak in my defence later,' he said, 'and let him talk without interruption.'

'I sure will,' Finlay said in a bored tone that suggested he hadn't bothered to listen to what Jeff had had to say and had already forgotten this instruction.

For once Ethan tried to catch Finlay's attention and demand that he act, but then trailed off. The next witness was Duggan Ward and he had already taken the stand. He was testifying and in mounting horror

Ethan's mind registered that he was providing the most damning evidence against him so far. Ethan listened in open-mouthed shock as he heard Duggan state that he'd seen Ethan acting strangely throughout the week. Ethan had often looked at the safe whenever it'd been opened, he reported, suggesting to him that he had been working out how to break into it.

'From then on,' Duggan said to the enraptured audience, 'I paid particular attention to Ethan's activities. So on the night before the raid I followed him. I saw him take a package back to his hotel. I didn't think anything of this incident at the time, but after the raid, I reported what I'd seen to Sheriff Fisher and only then did the truth come out.'

A murmuring went up as Duggan finished his testimony on an unresolved dramatic note, leaving the sheriff to finish the revelation.

'I looked under Ethan's bed,' Fisher reported when he'd taken the stand, 'and I found this.'

Fisher raised his hand and clutched in it was a substantial wad of bills. The audience's wail of righteous anger encouraged him to parade around on the spot waving the bills above his head while speaking loudly so everyone could hear him confirm they totalled nearly $1,000.

'His payoff,' Fisher said over the rising clamour from the enraged audience, 'for passing information on to Ansel Stark about the safe that helped him raid our town bank and steal our good citizens' hard-earned money.'

This evidence instigated a frenzied bout of angry fist-shaking from the watching audience and many raised loud demands for justice. Even the judge tutted to himself as if he'd heard enough already.

'I don't know nothing about that money,' Ethan whispered to Finlay, who nodded, again in a distracted manner as if he hadn't heard him. 'But Duggan Ward sure does. He was the one who got that payoff, except he planted it on me.'

Finlay still didn't react other than to grumble at Ethan to be quiet and let him compose his thoughts for his forthcoming defence.

Presently the prosecution ended their case and the judge asked Finlay to speak.

With a brief smile of encouragement to Ethan, Finlay stood. He looked around the court, buttoning up his jacket as he ensured he'd received everyone's full attention. He waited until complete quietness reigned in the courtroom.

Then he provided the case for the defence.

It was three words long.

'No further questions,' he said. Finlay then winked at Ethan and sat.

'Is that it?' Ethan whispered as the jury retired to consider their verdict.

'Don't worry,' Finlay said. 'If all the so-called evidence they have is that speculation and hearsay, they don't have a case. I've treated them with the contempt they deserve by not deigning to consider their meaningless babble as worthy of my consideration. My tactic is sure to work and the jury is sure to find you not guilty. Trust me on this.'

Ethan didn't trust anything Finlay had ever told him and so he wasn't at all surprised when the jury deliberated for less than five minutes before returning. The judge received their decision, looked down at him, and provided the verdict.

'Guilty on all counts,' he stated.

Pandemonium raged in the court-room for several minutes while the judge ineffectually banged his gavel in a forlorn attempt to regain control. When silence started to return, Ethan leaned towards Finlay.

'So much for trusting you,' he said.

'Still no need to worry,' Finlay said. 'You've still got that vital information they need to catch Ansel Stark. Without it you'd get fifteen years, but I reckon some judicious bargaining should get that down to five years, maybe even three.'

This time, Ethan decided to believe him. But as it turned out, nobody asked him about his vital information.

And he got twenty-five years.

5

Ethan passed the week after receiving his guilty verdict in a sombre and dejected state.

He was a man who liked his freedom. He'd roamed from Kansas to the shining mountains beyond the Missouri. For many years he hadn't had the ties of family and had devoted his time to enjoying the blue sky or the stars above his head and the miles passing beneath his horse's hoofs. The bustle of thousands of head of cattle had been his constant companion.

Now that life had gone and, considering the likely conditions he'd face in jail, possibly for ever. Even if he were to survive for long enough to gain his freedom he would spend the best years of his life eking out an existence in a small cell. The only time he'd spend outside would be when he suffered the back-breaking and soulless labour of rock-breaking.

His only remaining hope was that his attorney could resolve the miscarriage of justice even at this late stage, but Finlay Smallpiece left town shortly after the trial without seeing him again. So then, aside from the milling crowd that gathered outside the jailhouse to shout abuse for the first few days, nobody paid him any attention.

Even Jeff Tyler didn't come to visit him, but in his case Ethan guessed he was too embarrassed to face him. Sheriff Fisher spoke to him only the once to explain that he would have to remain in Bitter Creek for a while because he was so unimportant nobody could spare the time to escort him to jail. Apparently, someone would get the unenviable task later.

At the end of the week Maxwell Rogers, a morose and hunched individual, mooched into the jailhouse. Sheriff Fisher swore him in, then set out the terms for his employment, talking in a loud voice to ensure that Ethan would overhear him. Maxwell would receive $200 to escort Ethan to Leavenworth today. On completion of his task he'd receive another $200. Maxwell negotiated for $500, but was unsuccessful and so, in a dejected state, he took custody of Ethan.

They made their way to the train station through a mob of surly well-wishers. Once they were safely on the train, Maxwell led him to the end car. On the station side of the train people were venting their feelings by reaching up to bang the windows, so Maxwell turned his back on them and pushed Ethan down on to a seat on the opposite side to the station. Speaking tersely, he laid out his rules for Ethan's behaviour on the forthcoming journey.

'All I got to do is deliver your hide to jail and I get paid,' he said, eyeing Ethan with contempt. 'For the amount they're paying me it don't matter to me what state you're in when we get there. You try to escape, I shoot you. You move when I don't tell you to, I shoot you. You even breathe without asking permission, I shoot you.'

'Permission to breathe,' Ethan murmured.

'Granted. Now, don't talk again.'

When the train set off, Ethan complied with Maxwell's orders, but with Bitter Creek now behind him his thoughts turned to the fact that he didn't want to go to jail. If getting shot were to be the punishment for trying to escape, he reckoned it was a fate preferable to the slow death that awaited him. He judged that despite Maxwell's gruff demeanour he was a good man, so he had no intention of killing him, but that didn't change the fact that he needed to get away from his captor.

Clamped around Ethan's neck was a metal band with a chain that attached the band to his bound wrists. His feet were shackled. A three-foot chain connected his waist to Maxwell's left wrist. This level of confinement didn't give him much leeway to assault Maxwell, but he figured his main priority was to get his gun off him. Even encumbered he reckoned he could still aim it and shoot if necessary.

So he bided his time, waiting for the mistake that Maxwell would surely make. They'd set off late in the day on a journey that would encompass two nights. They would arrive in mid-afternoon of the third day.

The remainder of the first day passed without Ethan noticing an opportunity to act, but with only his consideration of Maxwell's behaviour to occupy his mind, as evening fell, he began to understand his captor's attitude.

Despite the bravado of his opening — and only — statement of intent, Maxwell was a nervous man. Clearly he had taken this assignment because of a desperate need for the money, and he just wanted to get it over with as quickly as possible. So throughout the evening Ethan feigned a relaxed state, aiming to lull him into a false sense of security, but this had no effect on someone who appeared to be permanently worried.

Maxwell had perched himself on the seat by the window in a position that kept him at the maximum distance he could get from Ethan. He always kept his gaze on him, and always kept his hand on the gun under his jacket at his hip.

When night came, Ethan let himself sleep, ensuring he got the rest that Maxwell would perhaps deny himself.

Deep into the night a sudden shake of the car awoke him, and he instantly snapped his head round to look at Maxwell. He found he was awake and staring at him, his hand beneath his jacket as always.

Maxwell smiled, clearly having stayed awake for just such an eventuality, but Ethan suppressed his own smile. If Maxwell wasn't even going to risk going to sleep on the journey to Leavenworth, he would be a tired and mistake-prone man before that journey ended.

Ethan slept soundly for the rest of that night. He did nothing untoward throughout the whole of the next day, letting his silence and relaxed demeanour do its own damage to Maxwell's nervous nature.

When the second, and final, night fell he was tempted to test Maxwell's frazzled nerves, but he resisted the temptation and after another good night's sleep he awoke to find Maxwell still staring at him. Now his escort was bleary-eyed, and his under-the-breath murmuring and the sweat on his brow suggested he was struggling to keep his concentration.

The morning introduced the last full day before they arrived in Leavenworth, so Ethan reckoned that the time when he'd have to force a situation was approaching. To further aid his cause the number of people in the car thinned out during the morning, leaving just seven potential witnesses to whatever he would have to do to escape. So as noon approached, he fine-tuned his plans, running through his actions in his mind. He didn't look at Maxwell, but instead listened to his breathing, hoping he might hear him slip into sleep after his lengthy vigil.

Around noon the train stopped and three passengers in their car alighted, only one joining the train, leaving just four witnesses, and all of those were giving them a wide berth. Ethan didn't reckon he'd get a better chance than this so, when the train set off, he steeled himself to make his move. He'd planned it carefully and it just required him to act quickly and assuredly.

He had been fidgeting all morning, looking as if he were trying and failing to get himself comfortable on the hard seat so as to get Maxwell used to him moving. His plan was that he would shuffle round, looking again as if he were about to shift his posture, but then swing towards his captor and hurl himself at him. He would need to gather a loop of the chain that connected them, then wrap that around

Maxwell's neck while with the other hand he got his gun off him. Maxwell would be sure to fight back, but Ethan reckoned that once he'd made his move he'd just have to keep going with it no matter what Maxwell did or who came to his aid.

He was building himself up to act when he saw that the only person to join the train had wandered over to their seat and was looking down at them with interest. Several people had done this over the course of their journey and each time Maxwell had ignored them until they went away.

The man introduced himself as Lansford Donner. Maxwell didn't repay the courtesy.

'What's he done?' Lansford asked, eyes gleaming with interest.

'Crime,' Maxwell replied eventually, his tone bored and in Ethan's opinion tired.

Maxwell's lack of interest didn't perturb Lansford and smiling now that he'd received a reaction, he pointed at Ethan.

'Sure has got to have been something mighty interesting for all those chains.'

'Nope.'

'We're a few hours from Leavenworth and it's sure to be a mighty boring journey. I'd like to hear that story, if you — '

'Go away,' Maxwell grunted, favouring him with an icy glare.

Lansford darted his head back with apparent hurt feelings.

'I was only thinking of you. You look terrible. But maybe if you ain't interested in talking, you should get yourself some entertainment.' He pointed over their shoulders at the door. 'There's a poker-game starting up in the second car and that has to be — '

'I ain't interested!' Maxwell snapped then darted a significant glance at his gun as his irritation finally got the better of him.

Lansford pouted with disappointment but then moved on to the other customers to extol the delights of the poker-game. This intrusion had the unfortunate effect of breaking Maxwell out of his previous lethargic state, so Ethan decided to postpone his escape attempt for a while. But when Lansford succeeded in persuading all but one of the passengers to check out the poker-game, Ethan couldn't help but smile despite the minor setback.

So, with only one witness to what he had to do, and that witness being a snoozing old man, Ethan prepared himself. He waited for fifteen minutes, by which time Maxwell had descended back into a semiconscious torpor.

He shuffled on the seat. Then he wrapped a handful of the chain around his wrist and lunged for Maxwell.

He managed to swing a loop of chain towards Maxwell's head before he reacted. But all sign of his lethargy disappeared in an instant as Maxwell sprang back to an alert state. With surprising speed he threw up a hand, catching the loop of chain before it could slap against his forehead. With his free hand he twitched for his holster, his gun coming to hand.

A sickness invaded Ethan's gut as he realized he was probably about to waste his only chance to escape on a futile skirmish, but he'd now committed himself. He heard the only passenger shout out a warning. Then feet pattered as the man ran for the door.

Ethan dismissed from his mind the fact that help would be only seconds away and changed his method of assault. He released the chain and lunged for Maxwell's gun, but Maxwell jerked back to press his back to the wall of the train, then swung the gun up to aim it at Ethan's guts.

From so close it was sure to blast a hole right through him, but Ethan didn't balk. Luckily Maxwell was at heart a decent man and despite his earlier threats he couldn't bring himself to fire. Ethan made him pay for that decency and clamped a hand down on the gun. He pushed the barrel away from his chest then tried to tear it away from Maxwell's grip.

Maxwell only gripped the gun more tightly and both men struggled for supremacy. The chains around Ethan's wrists hampered his movements and with him unable to brace himself Maxwell was able to push himself away from the wall. Then he bore down on him. Both men went sprawling over the seat with Maxwell on top, his flaring eyes and twisted grimace suggesting his momentary weakness had passed and now he'd have no compunction about shooting him.

Ethan strained but was unable to dislodge him and worse, he heard footfalls as at least one person returned to the car to help his captor. Ethan reckoned he had only brief moments to drag himself free of Maxwell's grasp and wrest the gun off him before his chance of escape disappeared for ever. So he gathered up his strength and shoved, hoping to dislodge him.

His effort made Maxwell buck slightly but then he bore down on him with even greater vigour, blasting all the air from his lungs. Worse, Ethan's grip of the gun slipped away. Out of the corner of his eye, he saw gunmetal glint as Maxwell dragged the weapon round to aim it down at his head while a shadow passed over him as the returning passenger hurried by the seat.

Ethan was almost ready to relent when Maxwell moved himself off him slightly, aiming to jab the gun up under his chin, but with space opening up between them a loop of chain happened to come to Ethan's hand. Ethan didn't question his luck: he gripped the chain, then flicked it at Maxwell's head. They were close and he couldn't deliver the blow with much momentum, but he managed to slap the chain across Maxwell's cheek.

Maxwell bleated, then flinched away, letting Ethan deliver a firmer blow with the chain that sent Maxwell falling off the seat. Maxwell hit the floor, almost dragging Ethan with him, but Ethan managed to keep himself on the seat and he saw and heard a clatter as the gun came free.

While Maxwell screeched in pain and clutched his face, blood oozing through his grasping fingers, Ethan slipped off the seat. He was aware that the returned man was watching him and that he was Lansford Donner, the man who had enticed everyone to leave to play a poker-game, but he put him from his mind. He darted his gaze around, looking for the gun and on his first sweep he saw it, lying just beyond Maxwell's sprawled body, four feet away.

Ethan threw himself forwards, his outstretched fingers brushing the metal before a firm and solid foot came slapping down on the gun, pinning it to the floor.

With a heavy heart Ethan looked up to see that Lansford had now reacted. Ethan braced himself, ready to rush him and prise the gun away, but Lansford must have seen the intent in his eyes because he clawed the gun backwards with his heel. The gun skittered away across the floor and far out of his reach.

Lansford fixed Ethan with his gaze.

'You're not shooting anyone today, Ethan,' he said.

The sudden question crossed Ethan's mind as to why Lansford knew his name when Maxwell had told him nothing about him, but by then Lansford had drawn his own gun. He aimed it down at him.

Ethan saw that his chance of escape had now gone and he rocked back on his heels, then knelt. He raised his hands as far as he could move them in a show of surrender.

On the floor beside him Maxwell stirred and looked up at Lansford.

'Obliged for your help,' he murmured, his fingers probing his face around the ragged cut where the chains had hit him.

Lansford ignored him and continued to glare at Ethan, his firm-jawed scowl and icy gaze giving Ethan the impression he was about to fire. Then

Lansford straightened his gun arm.

'No need to shoot,' Ethan said. 'I've given myself up.'

'Yeah,' Maxwell said from the floor. 'I can take care of — '

Lansford fired, the gunshot echoing in the small car.

Ethan flinched back, preparing himself for the pain to come, but then found himself tumbling to the floor with the chain that had connected his waist to Maxwell's wrist snaking wildly in the air. In a stunned moment he realized what had happened. Lansford hadn't shot him, but he had shot through his chains.

'Why?' Ethan murmured, but it was Maxwell who gathered Lansford's attention with his strident demand.

'What in tarnation are you doing?' he demanded. 'That's my prisoner.'

'He *was* your prisoner,' Lansford said.

'If you think you're getting your hands on my four hundred dollars, you're wrong. I've taken him most — '

'Be quiet!' Lansford glared at Maxwell until he clamped his mouth shut, then looked at Ethan. 'You with me?'

Ethan didn't need a second request or an explanation and he jumped to his feet, nodding eagerly.

Maxwell Rogers watched the sudden change in circumstance with growing anger reddening his face. Slowly he got his wits about him and levered himself to a sitting position. But almost as an afterthought Lansford swung his gun round in his grip then thudded the butt into Maxwell's temple, pole-axing him.

'That should keep him quiet,' Ethan said approvingly.

'And you need to keep quiet too,' Lansford said, pointing to the door at the end of the car. 'We haven't got the time to stand around talking.'

Ethan followed Lansford down the car, shuffling as fast as he could with shackled hands and feet. Already he could hear a commotion brewing behind him as others slipped into the car and tentatively edged forward as they tried to see what had happened. Ethan paid them no attention, not when for the first time the possibility of freedom was before him.

They slipped out the back door to stand before the rail. Below the tracks were trundling away from them at a pace that was fast enough to make the ground blur. They would have to jump to freedom and at the speed the train was travelling there was a strong possibility that a broken limb would result. Ethan hesitated, shuffling from foot to foot. Then, in the car behind him, he heard a cry of alarm as a passenger saw Maxwell's comatose body.

That was all the spur Ethan needed to move. He sat on the side rail, then swung his legs over. He looked down at the earth blurring along below him and braced himself to leap. He rocked his shoulders back and forth as he rehearsed the movements he would have to make. But he didn't get the chance to go through with his plan as

Lansford's firm blow slapped into the middle of his back and pushed him away from the rail.

Without control of his body Ethan flew through the air. An involuntary cry tore from his lips before he hit the ground on his side, blasting all the air from his chest. He rolled, going head over heels in a cloud of dust until he came to a scrambled halt and lay still, wondering whether he'd broken every bone in his body. Tentatively he shook himself, then sat. He flexed each limb, finding that despite the unplanned nature of his leap he had landed intact with his only damage being bruises.

He saw that Lansford was walking towards him, having already made his leap, batting the dust from his clothes and watching the receding train with interest. Ethan also swung round to watch it and confirm that aside from a few faces looking at him through the windows, nobody was showing too much interest and neither was the train showing any sign of stopping.

'You pushed me,' he said when Lansford reached him.

'Only because you were thinking about that leap too much,' Lansford said.

'Obliged.' Ethan gave a rueful smile. 'But only because it worked.'

Lansford acknowledged this with a curt nod as he halted before him.

'It's worked so far, but we've still got to get you to safety. I've got a base about two miles from the tracks.' He peered around, orientating himself. 'But you made your move sooner than I expected. I reckon it's still a few miles on.'

'Then we'd better set off.' Ethan got to his feet. 'But these shackles won't let me move quickly.'

Lansford backed away for a pace then signified how Ethan should stand for him to remove them. In short order he shot through Ethan's remaining bonds, letting him divest himself of the band around his neck, and the shackles around his wrists and feet.

The removal of the iron weight only helped to increase Ethan's pleasure at his freedom.

'Obliged again,' he said as they set off, going along broadly in the direction of the tracks but gradually moving away from them. 'But I've got to ask — why have you saved me?'

'I'll answer all your questions when we get to base.'

Ethan accepted this and stayed quiet as they walked. Presently the train moved out of sight, alleviating his concern that a pursuit would come soon and giving him greater hope that they'd reach safety. Lansford wasn't so optimistic and he set a blistering pace.

But nobody came looking for them and an hour later they reached his campsite. A single horse was there, along with provisions.

His saviour had already whetted Ethan's curiosity, but the fact that the belongings he saw were only for one man bemused Ethan even more. He had presumed Lansford must have had help to effect his rescue, but now it appeared as if he had made his way from here to the nearest station, presumably on foot. Then he had planned to get him off the train as near as possible to this site.

'All right,' Ethan said when they reached Lansford's horse. 'I'm impressed by what you did and mighty grateful, but I'd like to know now why you've saved me from a stretch in Leavenworth.'

Lansford gestured for Ethan to sit, which he did, then sat opposite him cross-legged. He drew his gun and spun the barrel, the action seeming to be a casual one, then he placed the gun on his lap before he spoke.

'I didn't save you from a stretch in Leavenworth,' he said. 'You're still heading there. You've just got a different person escorting you.'

Lansford swung the gun up to aim it at Ethan's chest and widened his eyes, all sign of his former jovial mood gone.

Ethan closed his eyes for a moment, surprising himself when he found he wasn't disappointed by this disastrous turn of events. He snorted a laugh.

'You have just got to be joking.'

'Nope. You and I are going to have ourselves a little talk and then we'll set off to complete Maxwell's journey.'

'I don't believe you. It sure has to look bad for you after you knocked out Maxwell and — '

'I've already worked out a story. Your captor will back it up after I've paid him off. You're the only one who'll suffer from that escape. You'll probably get another five years and one hell of a beating for your few hours of freedom.' Lansford snorted a humorous laugh. 'But it doesn't have to be that way. I could put in a word for you and make it sound like you never escaped, but only if you answer me one simple question: where is Ansel Stark?'

Ethan released a hearty laugh. 'You've wasted your time. I'm an innocent man. I sure ain't the bandit they say I am.'

'Don't believe that. Now talk.'

Lansford raised his eyebrows when Ethan didn't reply. 'I've been talking to some people back in Bitter Creek and I've heard you know where Ansel Stark went.'

'But that was weeks ago and . . . ' Ethan trailed off, deciding not to downgrade the information he had. Curiously, it hadn't bought him any leeway with the law, but maybe now his only bartering tool could help him, after all. He raised his chin and his voice. 'Yeah. I know where Ansel went, but the trouble is, I don't like your terms.'

Lansford smiled, as if he'd expected and hoped for this response.

'Then maybe I'll change the terms, for the worse . . . '

Lansford didn't continue with his threat, letting his firm gaze and silence let Ethan imagine what kind of punishment he would mete out if Ethan didn't comply. But Ethan had suffered plenty over the last few weeks and he found he didn't have the capacity in him to be scared. Instead, the only thing on his mind was the chance of escape that this current situation afforded him.

'What you want to know about him for? You some kind of bounty hunter?'

'I ask the questions.'

'I'm just wondering, because Ansel Stark must be worth plenty — five, seven, maybe ten thousand dollars by now. Me, I'm worth nothing, except for the information I have that'll get you to that ten thousand dollars.'

'It ain't that much and I'm not negotiating. Your reward for talking is you get to live long enough to die in jail. The only thing on your mind is how much you'll have to suffer before you talk.'

Ethan reckoned that without Lansford's intervention he might have succeeded in escaping from Maxwell, but that was after two days of resolute observation as he awaited the right time to act. He didn't have the same luxury in this situation. He needed to act quickly, and as the cold look in Lansford's eyes told him that defiance wouldn't work, he decided to try a different tactic.

He let his shoulders slump, heaved a resigned sigh, then shook his head while staring at the ground. Then he rolled forward until he was kneeling, raised his clutched hands to place them before his face, and begged for his life.

Two weeks ago, before his life took its terrible turn, he would never have believed he could be capable of doing such a thing, even if he was only pretending to be broken. In his current predicament he felt no shame. He wailed and sobbed and pleaded for Lansford to stop threatening him. He carried on begging long after his voice had become gruff. Every time Lansford spoke to utter his contempt for him he wailed even louder.

'That's enough!' Lansford roared at last over Ethan's protests and advanced on him with a hand raised. He cuffed Ethan about the cheeks and when

Ethan lowered his head, turtle-like, he slapped the top of his head and shoulders.

Still Ethan sobbed and in growing annoyance Lansford kicked him in the side, sending him tumbling to the ground. As if this last blow had knocked some sense into him, Ethan uttered a last snuffling sob, then quietened.

'I'm sorry,' he murmured, his voice faint and defeated. He levered himself up to a sitting position with a shaking hand, but still keeping his gaze locked on Lansford's boots. 'Things have been tough for me these last few weeks.'

'Then pull yourself together and start acting like a man or you'll never survive what's coming to you.'

With a pronounced shrug of the shoulders Ethan got himself under control and looked up at Lansford. He drew a last snuffling intake of breath, then nodded and swung his other hand round to push himself up to his feet. Then he stopped the movement to look at the hand. He flinched, seemingly noticing that it was shaking for the first time. Ethan flexed his fist several times then looked at it again. The shaking had stopped.

Ethan breathed a deep sigh of relief and shuffled round to get up. In the position in which he'd sat his legs were tangled up and so in his flustered state he failed to rise more than a few inches before tumbling back down to sit.

He gave a resigned shrug and held out a hand to Lansford to pull him up. With an unthinking reaction Lansford held out his hand. Ethan took it and quickly Lansford tugged him to his feet, but Ethan came up faster than Lansford had expected. All sign of his former defeated state had gone as he launched himself off the ground and hurled himself bodily at Lansford.

He hammered into Lansford's chest with a leading shoulder and knocked him back a pace, then kept driving himself on until he tumbled Lansford over. Lansford hit the ground. With his arms wheeling he rolled once and came to his feet, then danced away a few paces to avoid Ethan. He came to a halt looking back at him, but it was to face his own gun cocked and aimed at his chest.

All through the apparent crumbling of his spirit followed by the gradual process of getting himself under control Ethan had never stopped noting where the gun was, and when Lansford had fallen away he'd wrested it from his grasp.

'And now,' Ethan said, smiling, 'I think my plans have just changed.'

'You won't get away with this,' Lansford said, fury blazing from his eyes.

'Perhaps I won't, but right now I've got me a chance that not you nor nobody else was prepared to give me.'

Lansford sized Ethan up, then took a determined move towards him. Ethan nudged the gun downwards and tore off a shot that winged into the ground six inches from Lansford's right boot. Still Lansford advanced on him, so Ethan fired again. He'd aimed to halve the gap after his previous round but with Lansford moving quickly Ethan's aim wasn't good enough and the bullet ripped through Lansford's trouser leg, making him spin away, hopping.

'You lousy varmint,' Lansford grunted, rubbing his leg.

Blood oozed through the cloth and although Ethan hadn't intended to nick him, he firmed his jaw and sneered.

'That was your last warning. The next shot will take your kneecap off.'

Lansford slumped down to sit and nurse his injured leg. With him showing no further sign of defiance, Ethan backed away to the horse, always keeping the gun on Lansford. When he'd rolled into the saddle he tipped his hat.

'I'll track you down if it's the last thing I do,' Lansford muttered.

Ethan raised the reins but then lowered them in irritation.

'And you say that even though I'm leaving you alive, which is more than

I'd do if I were the man everyone reckons I am.'

'I don't care what sort of man you are,' Lansford snapped. He removed a kerchief from his pocket to wrap around his injured leg. 'I'll make you pay for this.'

'But you won't,' Ethan mused. 'You're not interested in me for any reason other than the information I have.' He looked around at the surrounding landscape, then pointed. 'See that rocky outcrop over there, about two miles away?'

Lansford ignored him while he wrapped the kerchief around his wound then looked towards it. He snorted.

'It's more like ten miles away.'

'Even better. Follow me there. You'll find some small rocks that'll form the shape of an arrow and that'll point you to a large flat rock. But be careful. It'll be in a cool spot so you'll have to raise it slowly to make sure it ain't got a rattler underneath.'

'Why should I do that when I've got

you to track down?'

'You're right. It will slow you down. Once you've walked there, found the arrow, then the right rock to look under, you'll have wasted a day, maybe more. But it'll be worth the effort because underneath you'll find a message about the only thing you want to know — the location of Ansel Stark's hideout.'

Ethan waited to see if Lansford would acknowledge this gesture, but he merely returned his gaze with surly anger.

'If you reckon that information will save your hide, you're wrong.'

Ethan raised the reins and hurried his horse away, leaving the cursing Lansford behind him.

'Trouble is,' he said to himself, 'I reckon you're right.'

6

For the two days after he'd escaped from Lansford's clutches Ethan slept little, kept moving constantly, and covered as many miles as he could. He took a convoluted route, doubling back and covering his tracks repeatedly so as to make it as hard as possible for Lansford to follow him.

But, though not knowing whether Lansford would muster sufficient motivation to come after him, Ethan was true to his word. He left him a note with 'Black Pass' written on it, the place he'd overheard that Ansel Stark would head to after the bank raid. So he presumed Lansford would go after the larger bounty the real bandit would provide him with.

His success in escaping from Lansford didn't cheer him. As far as the law was concerned he was a convicted bank robber on the run from justice. That meant other bounty hunters would come after him. Even if he could escape their clutches and stay one step ahead of the law, he could never return to the life he'd lived before.

That fact narrowed Ethan's choices as to what he did next. He couldn't move on without clearing his name. Although he had no idea how he could do that, he was sure of one thing: the evidence that had been presented at his trial had been mighty odd, as were the events leading up to the bank raid. There was only one place where he could find answers to these questions was: Bitter Creek.

Luckily, Bitter Creek was the last place anyone would expect him to go to. So Ethan reckoned it was a risk worth taking. Even so there was only one person in town who might be pleased to see him.

A week after escaping from Lansford, Ethan stood outside his target's house. It was late at night and darkness shrouded the small house, which was a mile outside of the town. A lamp inside lit the shutters, confirming that the house was occupied.

Ethan knocked on the door and as soon as it slipped open an inch he spoke.

'Don't be alarmed,' he said, 'I'm not here to cause you trouble.'

Jeff Tyler opened the door to look him up and down, his eyes wide, perhaps from the shock of seeing him. He darted his gaze past Ethan's shoulder to peer into the darkness before he beckoned him in.

'You'd better get in fast,' he said, speaking quickly and slapping him on the shoulder to usher him inside, 'before anyone chances to see you.'

Ethan sighed with relief as he went inside. In truth he'd had no idea what kind of reception he'd receive. Jeff was the only person to have spoken up for him at his trial, but such support didn't mean he wouldn't turn him in to the law in an instant. So he still kept him in view, noting his reactions, as he headed to the indicated chair and sat.

'You've probably heard about my escape,' he said.

'Sure.' Jeff sat in a chair opposite to him, but then rocked back and forth before standing. He paced before Ethan, nervously fingering his jaw. 'It was a daring bolt for freedom at gunpoint by a cunning bandit and his accomplice, according to Maxwell Rogers.'

Ethan snorted a rueful chuckle. 'That's not the way it happened.'

Jeff laughed, and as if that had helped to relieve his tension he sat again.

'I guess I already knew that. I wouldn't have let you in if I'd thought that what I'd heard about you was true. I know you're innocent.'

Ethan smiled, and finding that such a small reaction didn't please him enough he whooped a low laugh, then slapped his knee.

'That sure is great to hear.'

'Even if I'm the only person who believes it?'

'Even then, because maybe if you can tell me why you know I'm innocent, I might be able to prove it to everyone else.'

Jeff didn't reply immediately, his brow furrowing as if what he was about to say took a lot of effort.

'Because I was with you when we tried to find work with Sam Pringle's outfit, and I know what I saw out at Bluff Point . . . ' His serious tone trailed off as his voice became gruff. He coughed to clear his throat before he continued. 'And because I know Duggan Ward was lying and was the one who was really in cahoots with Ansel Stark.'

'How do you know that?'

Jeff raised his eyebrows. 'Two days after your trial he left town after breaking into the sheriff's office and stealing a thousand dollars, the evidence that helped convict you.'

'Where did he go?'

'He went north, from what I heard.'

Ethan nodded. 'Then maybe the law might be inclined to listen to the truth about him now.'

'Perhaps,' Jeff said with a sorry shake of the head that suggested he thought this unlikely. 'But what I guess nobody ever told you is that . . . is that Duggan is Sheriff Fisher's brother-in-law . . . and the judge's nephew.'

Ethan winced, seeing now why everyone had been so determined to prove his guilt and ignore the guilt of the obvious culprit.

'Then I've got no hope.'

Jeff offered a smile. 'You've got plenty of hope, but no certainties.'

Ethan considered his options and one thing was certain. He stood.

'Unless there's anything else you want to tell me, I'll be going.'

Jeff narrowed his eyes. 'Does your eagerness to leave mean you're going after Duggan?'

'Sure. Finding him and forcing him to tell the truth is the only chance I've got to clear my name.'

'Then stay here for a while. I'll ask around and see if I can find out more about where he went. A wanted man will find it hard to get that information.'

'No need,' Ethan said. 'I know exactly where Duggan's gone and I'll find him, bring him back, and make everyone accept what really happened here.'

'You won't,' Jeff said. He waited while Ethan furrowed his brow in confusion then slapped his legs and rose. 'Because we will find him.'

★ ★ ★

Five days after leaving Bitter Creek, Ethan and Jeff drew their horses to a halt on a small ridge overlooking the town of Black Pass. They had made good time in reaching this place and had managed to avoid contact with anyone. Although Jeff's decision to come with him had surprised Ethan, he hadn't questioned his reasoning. Not that Jeff encouraged chatter, staying quiet and grim-faced throughout their journey.

125

The town was a festering blot on the landscape. A rough collection of shacks nestling in a forgotten pass in the mountains, which wasn't on any trade routes or had any reason to exist other than one — nobody would ever normally visit such a place.

Ethan didn't expect that either Ansel Stark or Duggan Ward would still be here and he reckoned that Lansford Donner should also have passed through. He also expected that if the town deserved its reputation he stood little chance of persuading anyone to talk about Duggan. Despite this, it was the best place to start his quest.

Ethan turned to Jeff. 'If you want to stay out of town, that's fine with me.'

Jeff snorted a laugh. 'That's not you trying to talk me out of this like I tried with you, is it?'

'I wouldn't do that.' Ethan cast a significant glance at Jeff's Peacemaker. Jeff had bought the new weapon before leaving town and it sat on his hip in a manner that was so awkward it gave

Ethan the distinct impression he'd never fired a weapon before. 'But you're a . . . a placid man and I don't want you getting yourself killed over my problem.'

'I don't intend to.'

Ethan looked towards the town and he almost moved on without asking the one question that had burned in his mind ever since Jeff had agreed to come with him. Then he shrugged and asked it anyhow.

'Jeff,' he said, lightening his tone, 'why are you here?'

'To get — '

'And don't say to get Duggan Ward because I don't believe it.'

'But it is to get Duggan Ward . . . ' Jeff paused to shrug. 'And, if I'm honest, to show you how sorry I am.'

'You don't need to do that. You've been the only person who's spoken up for me.'

Jeff lowered his head. 'But I didn't convince anyone, and I did far less than perhaps I could have done if I hadn't been such a . . . such a yellow-belly.'

'I know it was hard for you to speak out in court when nobody wanted to hear what you had to say, especially when the person you needed to speak out about was the judge's nephew and the sheriff's brother-in-law.'

This comment didn't satisfy Jeff's need to wallow in self-pity and he gnawed at his bottom lip before he spoke again.

'There's more. I . . . I guess I knew Duggan Ward was up to no good all along. I just didn't want to face up to what it all meant, and you were the one who had to pay the price for my . . . my stupidity.' Jeff sighed long and hard. 'I've never told you the whole story about that first massacre out at the Clancy family home.'

Ethan narrowed his eyes. 'Then now might be the time.'

Jeff took his time in replying as he collected his thoughts.

'Duggan Ward was supposed to go out to the Clancy ranch to talk to

Eugene about his bank loan on the day the family was massacred. He left town but when he came back he said he'd never visited the place.'

'And people believed him?'

'They did. He was sweet on the Clancys' eldest daughter Lavinia but she didn't care for him and neither did her father. She used to sing in the saloon and he'd argued with her in there the day before. From what I heard, two strangers rode into town and she'd flirted with them. He didn't like it, but she wouldn't listen to him and the next day he claimed he couldn't get up the nerve to go see her and apologize. So I went out the next day instead to talk to Eugene . . . and found them all dead.'

'And now you reckon Duggan was lying and that he really went out there with Ansel Stark's bandit gang and paid her and the rest of her family back for rejecting him?'

'I do, and there's more. On the day of the second massacre, he also went out to Bluff Point. He said it was to visit the graves.'

Ethan ran through the tale in his mind, the pieces falling into place in a way that let him see the whole train of events in one terrible burst.

'Except you now reckon it was to lead Ansel to Sam Pringle's outfit because the two strangers who'd flirted with Lavinia Clancy were Isaac and Rory from the outfit?'

'That's the way I see it now. Ansel helped him kill the family out of anger for her rejecting him, and Sam Pringle's outfit out of jealousy. Ansel's payment was information on how to raid the bank.' Jeff shook his head. 'I'm just so ashamed I believed his story. I should have — '

Ethan raised a hand, silencing him, then smiled.

'Stop beating yourself up about this. I don't blame you for what happened.'

'But I do. It was my . . . ' Jeff hung his head, but then put a hand to his heart as he heaved an exaggerated sigh of relief. 'But I'm pleased to hear you don't blame me.'

Ethan blew out his cheeks, then pointed into town, effectively ending the debate. The two men set off towards town but, as if talking about his reasoning for coming on this quest had released a burden from his mind, Jeff relaxed enough to chatter openly for the first time. Unfortunately, now that he had voiced his main worry all his other worries assailed him and his voice broke several times as he questioned Ethan's decision to come to such a town. After they'd passed through the first line of rough shacks and faced the main road he flinched at every movement and sound, even when they were just leaves rustling by or a dog barking in the distance. By the time they dismounted outside the saloon, he was shaking.

'You need a drink,' Ethan said.

'More than I ever have.' Jeff rubbed at his face, even biting his hand in an attempt to regain control. 'But I can't do this. I just can't go in there. There might be — '

'You don't have to explain. Just stay here and keep lookout for trouble.' Ethan flashed a smile that Jeff didn't return. 'We might have to leave in a hurry.'

Jeff gulped as Ethan dismounted, but said nothing more. Ethan nudged through the batwings. From the corner of his eye he sized up the customers.

Several men sat in one corner, nursing empty glasses with studious concentration as they made an obvious show of ignoring him. One man lay stretched out on a bench with his hat pulled over his face. Two men were playing cards and didn't look his way. A quivering knife jabbed point down into a card in the centre of the table suggested they had more serious matters on their minds.

At the bar Ethan ordered a whiskey, feeling his neck burn from several guarded gazes. He threw a dollar on the bar then raised his voice to the bartender so that everyone could hear him.

'I wonder if an old friend of mine, Duggan Ward, has passed this way?'

The bartender shook his head, although as he'd started to grunt that he didn't know anything before Ethan had uttered two words of his question Ethan was minded not to believe him.

But Ethan wasn't interested in the bartender's reaction and with his glass clutched to his chest he turned and leaned back against the bar. None of the groups was looking his way, but the man who had apparently been asleep had swung his legs to the floor. He was now leaning back against the bench, but still with his hat pulled low over his eyes.

Ethan headed towards him and sat on a chair on the opposite side of a table, facing him. He considered him, silently.

'What do you want Duggan for?' the man said at last, his voice drawling beneath his hat.

'I've got money to give him,' Ethan said.

The man snorted with disbelief and raised his hat with an index finger. Lively blue eyes considered him.

'And you're a man who tracks other men down in places like Black Pass just to give them money, are you?'

'Only when they have something I want — information.'

The man's eyes narrowed with interest for the first time.

'And how much is this information worth?'

'A thousand dollars, five hundred now, five hundred when I know he ain't lied to me.'

The man nodded, his brief smile suggesting he did know Duggan Ward and knew this to be a worthwhile precaution.

'I don't care how much it's worth to Duggan Ward, only how much it's worth to me.'

'Fifty dollars.' Ethan watched the man sneer. He tried to hide his disappointment by firming his jaw. When he'd taken Lansford's horse he'd searched through the saddle-bags and Lansford had had a total of a hundred dollars on him. 'And another fifty dollars when you prove you ain't lied.'

'That's the right precaution to make with Duggan Ward, but you can trust Miguel Rico.' He slapped his chest and raised his chin, as if even the lowlifes in Black Pass had their pride. 'I'll take the hundred now.'

Ethan pondered while he met Miguel's stone-faced glare, then reached into his pocket and counted out the money on to the table. When Ethan sat back an eager smile twitched at the corners of Miguel's mouth. Miguel moved to grasp the wad, but Ethan slapped a hand on the bills first.

'Now take me to Duggan Ward.'

The sight of the money removed some of Miguel's truculence and he spread his hands in a gesture of benevolence.

'I'm an honest man so I'll tell you

this: I can't take you to him, only to a man who knows where he is.'

Ethan dragged his hand back, pulling the bills away.

'That's not good news.'

'It's the only news you'll get, and I can't take you to him if you keep that hand on the table.'

'I will raise my hand, but know this, one hundred dollars is all the both of you will get.'

Miguel fingered his moustache, the action covering a smile that acknowledged the game they were playing, one that was as filled with skill and bluff as any poker-game. The claim about the man who knew about Duggan was probably a ruse to get more money off him as he led him on a dance that would probably end with an ambush. But Ethan had showed he knew this and so Miguel was reconsidering, and as if he'd come to a final decision he lowered his voice and stood.

'All right,' he said, a matter-of-fact manner replacing his former playful tone. 'Come with me.'

'Where we going?'

'A place, about a mile out of town.'

Ethan noted that Miguel had spoken softly, but in the quiet saloon it was still at a level that any of the other customers would have been able to overhear. He picked up the bills and waved them at him before secreting them back in his pocket.

'Then the quicker we get there, the quicker you'll get these.'

Miguel headed for the door without speaking again. Ethan followed him.

Outside Jeff watched them leave with his eyes wide. Miguel paid him no attention as he mounted up and headed away from the saloon. Ethan mounted up, but didn't move off as he took the opportunity to tell Jeff what had happened. Throughout the brief summary, Jeff repeatedly looked to the receding Miguel, then to the saloon, shaking his head.

'Are you sure about this?' he asked when Ethan had finished.

'Yeah,' Ethan said. 'What's the problem?'

'Everything,' Jeff said, throwing his hands up in exasperation. 'I don't believe this man will do anything other than take us somewhere and steal our money, and perhaps even our lives.'

'There's a good chance that is what he's planning to do, but I have to take that chance and besides, he'll fail.'

'But he isn't the only one. What about the others in there? Somebody must have overheard you. And what about — ?'

'Jeff!' Ethan snapped in irritation, quietening his complaints. 'If you're that worried, like I've said, you don't have to join me.'

Jeff bit his bottom lip as he glanced around.

'I do,' he said, 'but we've got to start being equal partners in this venture, and I reckon this is a bad idea.'

Ethan was about to remind Jeff that he was the one who was trying to clear his name, but he had to admit that

Jeff's cautious view had merit.

'All right,' he said. 'Here's what we'll do. I reckon I can handle Miguel, so you stay here and watch the saloon. If anyone follows me, hightail it out of here and warn me.'

This change of plan met with Jeff's approval and so Ethan hurried his horse on, leaving Jeff outside the saloon. When he drew alongside Miguel, his new companion looked at him and gave a rueful snort.

'So,' he said, 'your friend is not coming?'

'He's staying to get himself a drink.'

'Or perhaps he's staying to ensure nobody follows us out of town.'

Ethan didn't reply to Miguel's latest move in their game of bluff and counterbluff, preferring to keep his concentration on the trail ahead in case the feared ambush was imminent.

At a steady pace Miguel led him on a trail that snaked out of town then uphill. Night was gathering, but he had a clear view of the town, so Ethan hoped Jeff would easily be able follow them if necessary. The shack Miguel was leading him to sat on a promonitory of rock looking down into the valley, only becoming visible when they were fifty yards away.

Immediately Miguel led him off the trail towards what appeared to be a sheer cliff face, although seen closer to, a vertical fault in the rock opened up that was just wider than a man. He led him into the dark interior and when Ethan's eyes became accustomed to the gloom he saw that the inside was wider than the entrance.

Miguel directed him to leave their horses under an overhang of rock that was just below the shack. This was a place that few knew about, Miguel reported, although Ethan was suspicious enough to see this comment as another part of Miguel's game that might or might not lead him to Duggan Ward.

They clambered up the side of a near-vertical stretch of rock to emerge level with the shack which, despite the gathering darkness, was unlit. Ethan gestured for Miguel to take the lead and enter the only door first and with a sly smile and a wink Miguel went inside.

Ethan waited outside, listening to Miguel rummage around inside. Presently a match flared and the light from a lamp glowed. Ethan peered through the only window, seeing that aside from a bundle of blankets the room was empty. He slipped inside and nodded towards the blankets.

'The man who knows where Duggan Ward is?' he asked.

'Sure.'

'And where is he now?'

Miguel shrugged. 'Who is to know?'

'You, if you want paid.'

'Perhaps we should just wait.' Miguel gestured to the floor, suggesting they both sit. 'I'm sure he'll return presently.'

Nothing about this situation felt right and Ethan ran his gaze around the room, taking in the door, the window, and then a second door, which he presumed led to another room.

'What's through there?' Ethan asked. He received a bored shrug from Miguel, so he took the oil-lamp over to the door. He backhanded the door open and peered into the darkened interior, then held the lamp inside, seeing into all four corners of the small, bare room.

Slowly he looped the toe of his boot behind the door then slipped it closed to see behind the door. The room was deserted, after all. Contented now that he had at least secured the inside he returned to the main room, but then stopped dead in his tracks.

Miguel had gone.

Ethan grunted with irritation. He heard feet patter outside as, presumably, Miguel embarked on his real mission of making off with his horse. Ethan hurried to the door, threw it open, then hurtled outside. He stopped, orientating himself and struggling to see in the darkness as he sought out Miguel. He couldn't see him but he presumed he'd already hurried down to the overhang where they'd left their horses. He set off. He'd managed a single pace when cold steel jabbed into his back and a man stepped forward to loom over him from behind.

'Miguel,' Ethan grunted, coming to a halt, 'you'd better not have double-crossed me.'

'I'm not Miguel,' a familiar voice muttered. 'And you'll keep those hands where I can see them.'

Ethan had no choice but to raise his hands as he spat out the name of his assailant.

'Lansford Donner.'

7

'So you're the man who can lead me to Duggan Ward, are you?' Ethan asked, keeping his voice calm.

Behind him Lansford grunted with irritation, then with a firm jab of the gun into his back directed him back into the house.

'Nope,' he said. 'I'm just here to get you.'

'For that nick to the leg?'

'For the information you have.' Lansford backed away a pace as the door opened and Miguel came back inside. 'This one doesn't know anything about Ansel Stark, but you do.'

With the gun no longer pressing into him Ethan took the opportunity to turn round. He saw Miguel raise his eyebrows, putting on a mocking shame-faced look as he considered him.

'Except here I am,' Ethan said,

'asking the same questions as you are. If I knew anything useful do you think I'd do that?'

'You'd better know something I can use because it's the only thing that's keeping you alive. Now answer my question or I'll blast you away.'

Ethan took his time in replying as he searched through the information he had to see if any of it might help Lansford. He had to admit his overhearing of this town being Ansel's destination after the Bitter Creek bank raid was the only useful fact he had.

'Blasting me away won't help you none, but keeping me alive might. We both want the same — '

'No deals. I'll find Ansel on my own.'

'I have no interest in the bounty. I just want to find these bandits to get hold of Duggan Ward and clear my name.' Lansford was glaring at him with undisguised anger, but Ethan kept talking. 'Surely the two of us can admit we have a common goal and work together on this.'

Lansford snorted his breath. 'I should have known I was wasting my time rescuing you from the train. Now I'm stuck here with no clues as to where to go next, and it seems to me that your usefulness ends here too.'

'I'm a resourceful man,' Ethan said, speaking quickly to keep Lansford's attention and keep him from firing, but Lansford was beyond reasoning with. He raised his gun to aim it squarely between Ethan's eyes.

'Last chance,' he said.

Nothing in Lansford's cold gaze gave Ethan any hope that he wouldn't fire. He opened and closed his mouth soundlessly as he fought to find something to say that might help him, but his mind remained blank.

A voice spoke from the shadows beyond the open door, breaking the tension-filled silence.

'Let Ethan speak.'

Lansford flinched, as did Ethan, and both men looked to the door. A man stood framed in the doorway as he stepped into the light, his gun drawn and aimed at Lansford's back — Jeff Tyler.

'Pursuit?' Ethan asked.

'Nope,' Jeff said. 'Just got twitchy on my own.'

'And has this twitchy man,' Lansford said, not moving his gun an inch, 'got the guts to pull that trigger? From what I've heard he ain't exactly suited to this kind of work.'

Jeff gulped. 'I'll guess there's only way I'll find that out. Except you won't live long enough to enjoy the truth.'

'But we don't want to do that,' Ethan said before Lansford could retort. 'We're all after the same people. I ain't saying we should join forces, but we shouldn't fight amongst ourselves. Lower that gun, Lansford. Then I'll tell you everything I know about Ansel Stark and you can tell me everything you know about Duggan Ward.'

Despite the reasonableness of the offer Lansford merely sneered and firmed his gun hand.

'Your friend has ten seconds to lower his gun or I will blast him too. Then you'll have ten seconds to start talking or you'll get the same.'

'Lansford, listen to sense. Jeff has a gun aimed at your back.'

'Aimed, yeah, but he's never killed a man before and the thought of that first time is tearing him up inside. I ain't got the same problem, and he's already used up five of those seconds.'

'It doesn't have to be this way. Three people have got to be better than one to take on the likes of Duggan Ward and Ansel Stark.'

Lansford started to shake his head, but over his shoulder Ethan saw Miguel do a double-take then peer through the window.

'Oh no,' Miguel murmured, 'that time has come all the sooner.'

Lansford stayed looking at Ethan for a long moment until Miguel's comment registered. Then he swirled round to face him.

'Ansel Stark?' he demanded, his eyes

gleaming with eagerness.

'I . . . I don't know,' Miguel said, peering into the darkness, 'but I reckon one of us got followed.'

Lansford kicked over the oil-lamp, extinguishing the light, then joined Miguel by the window. He cast a lingering look through the window, registering his disappointment with an oath, then ran for the door with Miguel trailing in his wake. He roughly barged Jeff aside before disappearing from view.

Ethan hurried across the room to join Jeff by the door and risked looking out. He couldn't see the people whom Miguel had apparently seen, but he heard the clop of hoofs from approaching riders and that was all the confirmation Ethan needed.

'This way,' he said, pointing then setting off. 'I left my — '

'I left mine there too,' Jeff said as they ran.

Without further discussion they scurried away from the house then made their way down the steep incline. Behind them Ethan heard the sounds the men made as they approached the house. Ethan had reached the bottom and was locating their horses when a cry went up. Ethan took that as a sign that their flight had been discovered.

That meant they had a lead of only a few minutes. Ethan moved towards his horse, planning to begin their flight as quickly as possible, but a hand emerged from the darkness and slapped down on his shoulder, stopping him. Another hand wrapped over his mouth.

'Be quiet,' Lansford grunted in his ear, 'you idiot.'

Ethan noted that Miguel had emerged from the darkness to accost Jeff and with no choice he meekly nodded and let Lansford drag him back into the darkness. They waited quietly for two minutes, hearing the sounds of men shouting beside the shack. Then horses thundered above them and continued on down the trail. They headed past the opening and disappeared from view. The group still waited quietly and presently three riders returned, heading back up the trail in their search for them.

'The only reason I didn't blast you to hell is that it'd have drawn their attention,' Lansford whispered in Ethan's ear. 'But maybe I should do that. One of those men could know where Ansel Stark is.'

Ethan didn't reply immediately as he listened to the men pass by on their search, but he did glance over to where Miguel was holding Jeff, and Miguel was grinning.

'You've already got that chance.' Ethan nodded at Miguel. 'He'll tell us where to go.'

'He don't know nothing about Ansel Stark.'

'He led those men to the house.'

'Hey,' Miguel muttered, releasing his hold of Jeff. 'Your idiot friend did that when they followed him from the saloon.'

Jeff frowned. 'Perhaps I did, but I

151

reckon Ethan is right. You're not to be trusted.'

Miguel rocked his head from side in a non-committed manner.

'Of course I'm not, but like Lansford said, I don't know nothing about Ansel Stark.'

'But you do know about another man.' Ethan raised his eyebrows. 'Duggan Ward.'

Miguel shook his head. 'I don't. Lansford asked me to look out for you and — '

'Quit lying,' Lansford grunted, showing an interest in this argument for the first time. He barged past Ethan and paced over to Miguel. 'What do you know about this Duggan Ward?'

'Nothing. It was just a ruse to get Ethan out here.'

Lansford looked Miguel up and down, sneering, giving Ethan the opportunity to speak up.

'He's lying. From the way he spoke about him, he's clearly met him.'

'For once in his worthless existence,'

Lansford grunted, 'Ethan has made a good point. Where is Duggan Ward?'

'I have no idea.' Miguel spread his hands in the same expansive gesture he'd used to Ethan. 'Trust me.'

All three men facing him snorted at once and in the ensuing silence Lansford considered him.

'But you have met him?'

Miguel took just too long in replying, his jaw moving as he weighed up his answer and this inactivity made Lansford draw his gun and sight him.

'I have,' Miguel murmured cautiously, eyeing the gun, 'but it was only the once and I — '

'Where did he go?'

'I don't know.' He considered the gun, which Lansford moved in to sight his head. 'Honestly, I don't know!'

'I don't believe you.' Lansford firmed his gun arm. 'So you've given me no choice but to shoot you.'

For long moments the two men looked at each other. Miguel was the first to break.

'All right,' he screeched. 'Maybe I do know where Duggan Ward went.'

'Then taking me to him will save your life.'

★ ★ ★

'I don't know who I trust the least,' Jeff said, 'Lansford or Miguel.'

Ethan snorted a wry chuckle. 'I reckon both of them have the same opinion of us.'

For the last four days the group had headed broadly northwards, riding ever higher into the mountains, the terrain becoming bleaker. Miguel, with Lansford always at his side, led them.

Lansford's surly attitude hadn't changed. He appeared as if he was unlikely ever to trust Ethan and Jeff, and he'd made it clear that he was only travelling with them because of a mutual need. Luckily, Miguel's presence had given him an alternative focus for his anger, and his failure to find any sign of either Ansel Stark or Duggan Ward had helped to ensure that his anger had grown by the day. Worse, the vagueness of Miguel's directions only gave more credence to the possibility that he'd bought himself time by promising to provide something he couldn't.

Jeff sighed. 'But what worries me the most is what Lansford will do if Miguel can't lead us to Duggan.'

'Then go. You've proved you had the guts to ride into Black Pass, and to keep your wits about you well enough to get away from those men. You've got nothing else to prove.'

Jeff shook his head. 'Except the only reason those men came after us is that they were following me.'

'You don't know that for sure.'

'I do. I waited in town like you said, but when nobody came out of the saloon, I started to worry and followed you, and — '

'Enough!' Ethan snapped. Since leaving Black Pass Jeff had repeatedly wallowed in self-pity over his role in this incident. He'd refused to accept he'd done the right thing in coming to his aid and preferred to brood about the terrible situation that could have come about because he might have been the one who had been followed. 'Just remember this — if you hadn't come, Lansford would have killed me.'

'It was pure luck that I happened to arrive at the right time, and I only came because I was worried about being on my own, not about you.'

Ethan considered Jeff, shaking his head. 'You're determined to think yourself a yellow-belly, but that's not the way I see you. Most times when a man is brave it happens because of luck or because he's just so plumb scared he doesn't know what he's doing. All that matters to me is that you arrived at the right time to stop Lansford.'

'Obliged for that, but — '

'No buts,' Ethan said, raising a hand. 'This beating yourself up ends here.'

Jeff gave a reluctant nod that suggested he might not continue to voice his concerns but they were still there.

'All right, but that doesn't resolve the other problem.' Jeff nodded forward to Lansford and Miguel. 'Lansford is convinced that Miguel has double-crossed him.'

'Lansford is convinced that everyone's double-crossed him.' Ethan sighed. 'And I reckon it won't be long before he stops keeping his cool.'

Jeff agreed, but Ethan's prediction came true faster than either of them expected. At noon they watered their horses at a spring and with the heavy clouds overhead suggesting rain was imminent, Lansford lit a fire to enjoy some hot food before moving on. Behind them was a monolithic outcropping of rock, towering above them like a giant finger, and around them the barren terrain formed a bowl. As soon as the fire was ablaze and smoking, Lansford voiced his irritation.

'Four days,' he grumbled, staring at Miguel through the flames, 'and still no sign of Duggan Ward. Where is he?'

'Just a little further,' Miguel said.

'You said that yesterday, and the day before, and the . . . '

Ethan cast an irritated glance at Lansford, who returned it with a wag of a finger that told him to stay out of this. Ethan lowered his head in exasperation. Conversations such as this one had started every day and they always descended into arguments and recriminations.

'He went that way,' Miguel said in a resigned tone, gesturing towards the ridge ahead.

'Did he?' Lansford licked his lips, savouring his next comment before he made it. 'Was that that way the first time, or the second time?'

Miguel gulped. 'I don't know what you mean.'

'You do. You're leading us around in circles.'

This comment caught Ethan's attention and he snapped round to look at Lansford.

158

'How do you know that?' he asked.

Lansford pointed to the rock formation towering above them.

'Because I saw that rock yesterday, except it was behind me. Clouds have kept the sun away so it's hard to keep a bearing, but I've been looking for landmarks and I've seen this rock before.'

In a fluent gesture Lansford drew his gun and sighted Miguel.

'You won't shoot me,' Miguel murmured. 'I'm your only chance of finding Duggan.'

Lansford grinned and raised his eyebrows.

'Lansford,' Ethan said, standing, 'stop threatening him and let's talk about this.'

'We are talking. Miguel is now going to tell me the truth. He's going to tell me why he's leading us in circles. Then, after he's told me where the trap he's leading us into will be sprung, he's going to tell me if he really knows where Duggan is. Then he's going to take me to him, and he's going to do it now.'

'And if he doesn't answer?'

'Then he dies.'

Ethan looked skyward. 'Enough, Lansford. You keep on drawing guns on all of us, but you never shoot anyone. Perhaps if you weren't making us all so fraught, we might make some progress.'

Lansford flicked his gaze away from its sneering appraisal of Miguel.

'You saying I ain't got the guts to shoot him?'

'I'm saying even you aren't fool enough to destroy our only chance of finding Duggan.'

Lansford considered him, then shrugged. 'Nice try at deflecting my anger, Ethan, but Miguel is leading us into a trap and this argument is between him and me. Now talk, Miguel, why are you leading us around in circles?'

'I'm not,' Miguel said.

Miguel met Lansford's gaze. Whereas the previous time when they'd confronted each other at gunpoint Miguel had relented and looked away, this time he didn't. Lansford flared his nostrils then looked away to consider the rock, running his gaze up and down it. Then he turned back to Miguel and narrowed his eyes.

'I have seen that rock before,' he said, his voice low and menacing. 'Last chance, Miguel. Talk!'

Miguel must have detected the change in Lansford's tone because he swallowed heavily, but he still gave a barely perceptible shake of the head.

Lansford's right eye twitched. Then he pulled the trigger. The explosion of gunfire echoed as lead blasted Miguel in the chest and sent him spinning to the ground.

Lansford stood. He looked down at Miguel's writhing body then cast a warning glance at Ethan and Jeff. He shook his head, but Jeff ignored him and hurried to Miguel's side. Ethan wavered, torn between believing Lansford's claim and helping the wounded man.

As he looked around the surrounding terrain he had to admit Lansford could be right. Miguel could have led them in circles and this place was an ideal location for an ambush. Looming rocks surrounded them, providing an assailant with plenty of cover. But when Miguel groaned in pain he put aside his concerns and hurried to Jeff's side. He slapped a hand on his shoulder as he sat beside Miguel, but saw there was little they could for him. The bullet had torn into his flesh and blood was drenching his shirt already.

Ethan heard footfalls behind him and turned to see Lansford advancing on them. He stood to face him, ready now to confront him, but Lansford batted him away.

'What's your plan?' Lansford grunted, standing over Miguel.

Miguel didn't reply for a few moments. Filmy anguish glazed his eyes and when he did speak, his voice was low and pained.

'Got no plan. Just . . . Just . . . '

'Spit it out.'

'Lansford,' Ethan snapped, 'leave him alone.'

Lansford moved back a pace to keep Ethan in his view.

'You even consider moving for your gun and you'll be dead before you complete that thought. Now talk, Miguel. What have you done?'

A pained smile crossed Miguel's face.

'All right,' he said. 'You're right. I've led you as far as I can. It's a trap as much as you want it to be.'

Lansford gestured around at the surrounding landscape.

'Explain!'

'Before you shot me I really was trying to get you to Duggan . . . ' A bolt of pain contorted Miguel's face. 'It's like this: few people know where Ansel Stark's hideout is. Only the people he trusts come and go. The rest wait to be led in, and only then when they're blindfolded.'

'I thought you were one of the trusted ones.'

'You should have realized that Ansel wouldn't have trusted the kind of people who would talk to you with the knowledge of where his hideout is.'

'But it's close? Near to this outcrop?'

'From what I have heard, but you could roam for months in these crevices and peaks and never find it. So find Duggan Ward and follow him in.'

'And where is he?'

'Who's to know?' Miguel murmured, his voice growing faint.

'You, if you want to live ... ' Lansford waited for Miguel to reply and when he didn't he shrugged, then blasted lead down into his chest.

Miguel twitched but Lansford continued firing, loosing four bullets into his sprawled form. Only Ethan slamming a hand down on his arm stopped him from continuing.

'He's dead,' Ethan said. 'Stop it!'

'I know,' Lansford grunted, throwing Ethan's hand away, 'but I never leave problems behind me.'

'He was no problem. He didn't lead

164

us into a trap. He just brought us as far as he could and if you hadn't have confronted him, he might have explained what he was — '

'Be quiet! Nobody takes me for a fool or keeps me from Ansel Stark.' Lansford swung round to face him, anger darkening his face and bloodlust blazing from his eyes.

'Surely Ansel Stark's bounty ain't enough for you to kill a — '

Lansford roared with anger, then advanced on Ethan and swung a pile-driving fist at him. Ethan tried to duck away from it but even so the fist caught him a glancing blow to the cheek that was powerful enough to wheel him to the ground. Ethan ploughed into the dirt before coming to a shuddering halt on his back, his senses too jarred to do anything but look upwards until Jeff swung into view, looking down at him.

Jeff helped him to a sitting position, and by now Lansford had left them and had mounted his horse. Then he set off towards the ridge ahead. He didn't speak again or look back.

'Like you say,' Jeff said, 'he sure does want that bounty mighty bad.'

'Beyond all reason,' Ethan murmured, probing his cheek.

'And that leaves us with a problem. Follow him or make our own way.'

Ethan looked around, weighing up their options as he gathered his senses.

'The way I see it, Lansford doesn't know any more than we do about where this hideout is, and his chances of finding Duggan are just as good as ours are.'

'So we should search for ourselves.'

'Perhaps, but for now Lansford has had the right idea. We need to leave here in case Miguel has led us into a trap, after all.'

Jeff agreed to this and so, after giving Miguel the dignity of dragging him out of sight, they set off, following on behind Lansford. They aimed to keep some distance on him, but they need not have worried as Lansford set a severe pace, pushing his mount to scramble up the slope ahead and he quickly headed over the top of the ridge. The more cautious Jeff and Ethan took twice as long to reach the summit. When they looked over the top a wide plateau lay before them and Lansford was nowhere to be seen.

'Which way do you reckon he went?' Jeff asked, staring at the hard ground as if he might pick up signs of Lansford's passage.

'I don't know,' Ethan said, 'but he must have worked out where he'd head to next quickly, and that means it ought to be obvious.'

Jeff joined Ethan in peering around but the barren landscape ahead was free of obvious destinations. They could set off in any one of a dozen different directions and each one was equally unpromising.

'We don't have to make any sudden decisions, but I'd prefer to get down from this high-up position. We might not be able to see anything, but up here others might see us.'

Ethan readily agreed to this plan and they made their way over the plateau. When they reached the other side a pass trailed down ahead, which would take them to lower ground and although they couldn't see Lansford they decided this was as good a route as any. As they made their way down, Jeff's last comment niggled at Ethan's mind with an uneasiness that was beyond the possibility that other people could be watching them. They'd reached the bottom when Ethan identified his concern.

'We're wondering how we'll find Duggan,' he said, 'but maybe we won't have to. All that gunfire might draw him to us.'

'Yeah,' Jeff mused, 'Lansford reckoned Miguel had led us into a trap and yet he lit a fire, and then he was mighty keen to get away and leave us after he'd shot Miguel to pieces.'

The final piece of Ethan's concern hit him.

'Remember Lansford's comment to me before he hit me,' he said, drawing his horse to a halt.

'He said something about not leaving his problems behind him.'

'And we're a problem. If he'd been as ruthless with us as he'd been with Miguel, he'd have killed us, except he left us, and quickly. I'm guessing that wasn't due to no benevolent spirit.'

Jeff gulped. 'He's used us. He's hoping the smoke and the gunfire followed by us riding along in full view will draw Duggan Ward out.'

The two men looked at each other, both frozen in a moment of accepting the shocking truth. Then both their gazes turned to look for the nearest cover. The pass was boulder-strewn and provided them with plenty of places to hide, but it also gave any assailant plenty of cover too. Ethan suppressed a shiver as he imagined many pairs of eyes looking down at them as they picked their moment to attack. Luckily 400 yards ahead the pass fell away sharply, suggesting safety might lie there.

'Don't do nothing to get anybody who's watching excited,' Ethan said. 'We'll just carry on riding to that edge. Then we get down and find somewhere to hide.'

Jeff grunted his agreement to this plan and they rode on. The back of Ethan's neck burned, as if someone was targeting him. Beside him Jeff was doing his best to ride on in an unconcerned manner but he was also darting his gaze around. That persuaded Ethan to draw his horse to a halt.

'What you doing?' Jeff demanded.

'You're just looking too worried.' Ethan considered the edge of the pass, still fifty yards ahead, a distance that might as well be fifty miles if an attack was imminent. Trying to appear casual he swung down from his horse. 'We head for cover now.'

Jeff nodded then cast a last long look around before he jumped down from his horse.

'But where will be — ?' Jeff didn't get to finish his question as a gunshot blasted, kicking dust two feet away from Ethan's right boot.

That was all the encouragement either man required to run for cover as an echoing volley of gunshots peppered around them.

8

Ethan pounded across the ground with bullets kicking grit at his heels, then hurled himself to the ground before rolling into cover behind a large boulder. Jeff skidded on his side into cover beside him. Then both men scrambled round to put their backs to the boulder and take stock of their situation.

'You see where that shooting's coming from?' Ethan asked.

'It sounded as if it came from everywhere,' Jeff said.

Ethan turned and ventured to rise a few inches, but the mere exposure of his hat poking out above the boulder provoked a burst of lead that scythed into the rock and forced him to duck down again.

'Seems it does come from everywhere. But who is it? Duggan Ward, or was Lansford right and Miguel was leading us into a trap?'

'I reckon it is Duggan. I think Miguel was being honest to an extent.' Jeff shrugged. 'But does it matter when we're this outnumbered?'

'Maybe not, but if it is Duggan, we might be able to talk with him.' Ethan smiled, feigning a confidence he didn't feel. 'And find out what we're up against.'

'Then talk away.'

'Duggan,' Ethan shouted, his voice echoing in the pass, 'your old friend Jeff Tyler is here and I'm sure you don't want to kill him.'

Jeff gave a sorry shake of the head that said this line of approach wouldn't work, but to Ethan's surprise Duggan shouted out.

'Jeff sure wasn't no friend of mine,' he said, his voice coming from half-way up the ridge on the opposite side to them, 'and neither are you.'

'Forget Jeff,' Ethan shouted. 'This is just between the two of us.'

'It ain't, and there is just the two of you. I've got plenty more men here. You don't stand a chance.'

'If you think that, you'll just have to come and get us.'

With that comment Ethan slumped down and with his back to the boulder he ran his gaze up the side of the pass above them. Unlike the time in Bluff Point where he and Jeff had used the cover to escape undetected, this time boulders were strewn with gaps of more than ten yards. It would need a huge amount of luck to survive the trip from one to the next and they certainly couldn't sneak away unseen.

Jeff noted Ethan's glum perusal of their chances.

'So what do we do?' he asked.

'Our best hope is to do nothing. We sit here and wait them out.'

Jeff shook his head at the unlikelihood of this plan working.

'What about trying to get over the edge of the pass like we'd planned to do?'

'It's fifty yards away. You reckon we can get that far?'

Jeff frowned and as he couldn't provide any other option he had no choice but to agree to wait.

For the next hour Duggan shouted taunts at them but they had no impact on men who were playing a waiting game. To that end sundown was still several hours away at which time they might be able to sneak away. Ethan put his faith in Duggan being someone who was too cautious to make a quick move and for a while that plan worked. But as the shadows lengthened down the pass, Ethan heard the scrambling sounds of men moving to closer positions.

'Get ready,' he whispered to Jeff then rolled round to squat on his haunches.

Out in the pass he heard muffled orders, then more scrambling, this time closer to. Ethan jumped up to be greeted with the sight of four men hurrying across the pass in pairs, both pairs aiming to outflank them. The pair to the right was heading towards higher ground while the ones on the left were skirting along the edge of the slope where the pass dropped away suddenly.

Ethan aimed at the pair to the right and fired, blasting one man in the chest and sending him ploughing head first into the dirt. He took a bead on the second man, but that man dived to the ground and with a low profile returned fire. That shot winged several yards wide and Ethan risked staying exposed and returned fire.

To his side Jeff had also stood. He aimed and fired at the second pair. From the corner of his eye Ethan saw one man throw up his arms before stumbling to his knees, then tipping over the edge to disappear from view. The second man wheeled away clutching his chest to land on his side, then slowly slipped out of sight. Then the man who'd gone to ground bucked before rolling away to lie on his back.

With all four taken care of, Ethan and Jeff ducked down.

'Nice shooting, Jeff,' Ethan said,

slapping his shoulder.

'That wasn't me,' Jeff said. 'They all got shot in the back.'

'Lansford!' they both murmured together.

'Well,' Ethan said, 'I guess if he was going to use us to draw Duggan out, at least he had the decency to help us.'

Another volley of gunfire blasted out in the pass and Ethan bobbed up. He saw dirt kicking up from gunfire on the facing slope. He couldn't see the people trading fire but he judged that Duggan's group was about twenty yards up the slope to his right and Lansford was towards the bottom of the slope. Ethan and Jeff joined in, helping Lansford by firing at Duggan's group. They had no targets to aim at but with their sustained gunfire pinning them down, Lansford had greater luck.

One man cried out before standing upright and tumbling into view, then rolling down the slope until he slammed to a halt in a cloud of dust. A second man took flight. He flashed in and out of view behind boulders as he made his away up the pass, but a bullet in the back brought him to a halt and he slid to the bottom of the pass on his belly.

Then the gunfire was all in one direction from Lansford until that too petered out. Several minutes passed in which Ethan and Jeff darted glances at each other, debating whether the fight was over before Lansford again started firing. At first Ethan couldn't tell what he was shooting at until he saw a flash of colour moving, resolving it into being a man high up in the pass who was aiming to escape over the top of the ridge. From such a distance Lansford's gunfire failed to find its target and the man slipped over the top.

But as he disappeared from view Ethan did have one final sight of the man, and this man had bright ginger hair.

'Duggan's got away,' he murmured, slapping the boulder before him in irritation.

'Yeah,' Jeff said, 'but at least the rest didn't.'

Cautiously both men stood and paced out into the pass. They'd reached the first group of bodies before Lansford stood up. He walked sideways while looking up his side of the pass until he joined them.

Ethan had mixed emotions. He was annoyed at having been used to draw Duggan out, but also felt a touch of gratitude that Lansford had saved them. He limited his expression of those conflicting thoughts to one word.

'Obliged.'

'Don't be,' Lansford said, looking towards the position where Duggan had disappeared. 'That Duggan Ward got away.'

'Then we just have to follow him and — '

'We got to do nothing. Your use to me has now ended.' Lansford snorted. 'Drawing gunfire is the only thing you can do right.'

'Maybe you're right, but three of us

have got to be — '

'Be quiet!' Lansford roared turning to face him. 'Men who ain't no use to me no more end up dead. Just be grateful — '

A gunshot sounded, kicking dirt to Ethan's right. Ethan flinched, then looked up the pass. Far up he could see Duggan peering over the top of the ridge.

'Get down!' he shouted.

Lansford spun round as Ethan and Jeff went to ground. He took a sighting on Duggan's distant form but he didn't get to fire, instead wheeling to the ground as a gunshot tore into his side, the report sounding a moment later. Then Duggan turned on his heel and hurried away.

Although Ethan felt no anger at seeing Lansford go down, his anger at Duggan finally brimmed over and without comment to Jeff he hurried to the slope.

Jeff shouted at him to not be foolish, but he ignored him and clambered up the side of the pass to reach the top of the ridge, peering over it less than two minutes after Duggan had shot Lansford. Duggan had gone, and even after he cautiously scouted around, he couldn't find him.

Ethan considered widening his search, but decided to return to Jeff and get his help. When he started making his way down into the pass he saw Jeff kneeling beside Lansford's form. Still without feeling anything but disgust for Lansford and his methods he reached ground level.

'How is he?' he asked as he approached them.

'He don't look good,' Jeff said, now loitering a few yards away from Lansford, the sneer on his face suggesting an argument had just taken place.

Ethan knelt beside the injured man. 'What do you want us to do?'

Lansford slapped his hands to the ground and strained to move himself, but failed.

'Go to my horse,' he said, gritting his

teeth against the pain. 'Get me my saddle-bag.'

Ethan did as requested. He flipped the bag open as he resumed his position at his side.

'What do you want from — ?'

'Give it to me,' Lansford snapped.

Ethan held the bag out, letting Lansford snatch it from his grasp. He lay with it held to his chest, taking deep breaths.

'I know you don't want our help, but you've been shot in the side and unless you accept it, you're going to die up here.'

'I know that.' Lansford clawed at the ground, trying to move himself, then relented. 'Get me sitting.'

Ethan glanced at Jeff, encouraging him to approach and with each man taking an arm, they dragged him to the side of the pass where they propped him up against a boulder.

Lansford grunted several times with the pain as they moved him, but he kept the bag clutched to his chest as if it would save him. When they'd moved back from him, he swung it open. He fished inside, but another spasm of pain contorted his face and he relented, letting his head fall back to rest on the boulder. The bag slipped from his grasp to lie on its side, its contents spilling out.

'What you want from in there?' Ethan asked using the friendliest tone he could muster.

'In a white kerchief,' Lansford gasped, a resigned tone replacing his former truculent attitude.

Ethan did as requested, finding a rolled-up kerchief. Inside was a small, cold object, a golden sheen shining through the thin cloth. He had expected to be looking for a knife to remove the bullet or perhaps medicine for the pain, and he looked at Lansford. He received an affirmative grunt so he placed the kerchief in Lansford's hand, then stepped back.

Jeff and he exchanged a bemused glance as Lansford opened the cloth to reveal a locket, which he flicked open with a fingernail. Inside was a picture of a woman's face. With his other hand Lansford fingered the portrait, closing his eyes as he traced over the picture, as if he could imagine he was touching the actual person.

'You finished gawking at me?' he said when he opened his eyes.

'We're sorry to intrude,' Ethan said, 'but if we're going to get you to some help we need — '

'No help. I'm dying.'

Ethan didn't bother denying this and although he didn't want to annoy a dying man, he asked the question he felt he ought to ask.

'Who is she?'

'Was,' Lansford murmured. 'She was my wife.'

'She was a right pretty woman. You must have cared for her greatly.'

'That caring will only end when I die.'

Lansford looked up at him with pain in his eyes, and it was beyond the pure physical pain he was suffering, giving Ethan a hint as to why this man had been so ruthless.

'When did she die?'

'Two years ago. You don't need to ask the rest. Even you must have worked it out.'

Ethan lowered his head in embarrassment because until now he hadn't. He'd assumed Lansford was a bounty hunter when he'd wrested him from Maxwell Rogers's clutches and he'd never reconsidered that belief. Now he understood the truth.

'Ansel Stark killed her,' he said.

Lansford gave a barely perceptible nod as he gazed at the locket.

'I came home. His heathen horde had ransacked the house and took her. I never found her body.' Lansford breathed deeply, perhaps suppressing a sob. 'Never could give her a decent burial. She'll have lain somewhere, like I will, mouldering and forgotten.'

'This won't be a comfort, but I have to find Duggan Ward to clear my name and so I guess I'll come up against Ansel Stark. I promise you — '

'Don't!' Lansford snapped, suddenly gathering enough strength to snap round and glare at Ethan. 'Don't make no promises to a dying man.'

'I've got no problem making that promise to you.'

'Don't do it for me. Don't do it for yourself.'

'What you mean?'

Lansford considered Ethan and gradually the harsh lines around his eyes smoothed and he relaxed back against the boulder. When he spoke his voice was softer than it had ever been before.

'Ethan, I got some advice. Give up on Duggan Ward and Ansel Stark and the rest. You want to clear your name, but forget it. This is a big country with enough land for any man to start afresh. I couldn't, but maybe . . . maybe I should have done. Forever chasing after Ansel destroyed the man Mary knew. Don't let the same happen to you.'

After hearing this impassioned speech Ethan didn't think he could do anything but nod.

'I won't,' he said.

'Now leave me to die in peace with Mary,' Lansford said. Without looking at Ethan again he drew the locket up to his face and stared at it, filling his field of vision with the only image he wanted to see.

Ethan and Jeff turned their backs on him and retired to a respectful distance away. Neither man looked back at Lansford or spoke. Time passed slowly until presently Ethan heard a muffled thud followed by a faint tinkling. He turned to see that Lansford was lying on his side with his hand outstretched. The locket had rolled free and was spinning slowly to a halt, the low sun's reflected light casting shimmering echoes of the woman he'd once known across Lansford's face.

Although Ethan was minded to just leave Lansford's body where it lay, after he'd shown some humanity at the end he didn't feel that that was appropriate. Jeff readily agreed and so they dragged Lansford to the edge of the slope.

Twenty feet below, two of the men Lansford had shot had come to rest and although they'd have liked to have moved them, the route down was treacherous. So they ignored them and set about gathering rocks to pile over Lansford's body.

The sun was edging below the peaks to their right when they deemed the job complete. They stood over the grave, both men searching for something appropriate to say. Jeff was the first to find his voice.

'Get some peace, Lansford,' he said.

Ethan could think of nothing to say about a man whom he'd hated throughout the short time he'd known him. He stood silently for two minutes then turned to Jeff and nodded towards his horse.

'Time to go.'

Jeff nodded. 'You didn't make him a promise but I assume we're still going after Duggan Ward?'

'Sure.'

'And Ansel too?'

'Sure.'

'If we get the chance, it'd be nice to find out where he dumped Mary's body.' Jeff gulped. 'And for that matter the Clancy girls' bodies too. Nobody deserves to go like that, unmourned and unremembered.'

'We'll remember,' Ethan said, 'for all of them.'

They slapped their hats on their heads and turned to pace soberly towards their horses. But after two paces both men stomped to a halt. Ethan rocked back in surprise, not believing for a moment what he was seeing.

Duggan Ward was standing before them.

Ethan flinched for his gun but a confident shake of the head from Duggan halted his hand.

'I've returned with a whole heap of guns to get you, Ethan,' he said. 'Don't complete that move if you want to live.'

Ethan raised his hand slightly. 'Why you got so many men with you? You aiming to bolster Ansel Stark's forces?'

'Something like that.'

Ethan glanced around, trying to pick out where Duggan's purported guns were hiding. He saw no sign of anyone, although with there being so many hiding places he was inclined to believe they were out there.

'What do you want with us?'

'I have the same question. You, I can understand, but not Jeff.'

'My reasoning,' Jeff said, 'is the same as Ethan's.'

'Is it?' Duggan murmured, rocking his head to one side as he considered him.

Jeff swallowed, then backed away to stand beside the grave.

'It is. You lied about what happened back in Bitter Creek and a good man like Ethan is now a wanted man. Another good man lies dead here.'

Duggan darted his gaze down to

consider the grave.

'So you hired a gunslinger to get me.'

'He was no gunslinger.'

Duggan gave a barely perceptible shrug, effectively dismissing Lansford from his consideration.

'Neither are you, Jeff.'

'I never claimed to be.'

'And Ethan is fool enough to trust the man you're claiming to be, is he?'

Jeff lowered his head and when Ethan looked at him, wondering what Duggan had meant, he didn't return his gaze. As nobody spoke, Duggan raised a hand and gestured. This must have been a prearranged signal because a man stepped into view from the side of the pass. Then one by one others appeared from out of their hiding places.

Ethan and Jeff were hopelessly outnumbered and when Duggan signified that both men should throw their guns to the ground, any chance of mounting a defence disappeared.

'What you reckon we do?' Ethan asked, speaking quietly from the corner of his mouth. Jeff didn't reply, so Ethan grunted out his question with more urgency. 'Jeff, what you reckon?'

Several seconds passed until, with a start as if he'd been pondering on a difficult problem, Jeff snapped round to look at Ethan.

'We have to get away,' he whispered.

'I can see that,' Ethan said, eyeing the steadily approaching line of men. 'But how?'

'Don't look back. Just count to five then turn, run and leap.'

Despite the order to not look back, Ethan couldn't help but flick his gaze back at the edge of the pass. Ethan thought back to what he'd seen over the side while they'd been burying Lansford. All he could remember was a steep slope, jagged rocks sprawled down a long drop to ground level, and the bodies of the men Lansford had shot lying about twenty feet down the slope.

'There has to be another way,' he said.

'Three . . . ' Jeff whispered. 'Four . . . '

'Jeff!'

Jeff murmured the end of his count then did as he'd suggested. He turned and ran.

Ethan hesitated, seeing Duggan flinch in surprise then throw his hand to his gun. Thirty yards behind him, the line of men halted, the nearest two throwing their gun arms up to aim at Jeff's fleeing form. That was all the encouragement Ethan needed. He turned and ran, seeing Jeff reach the edge then throw himself over the side, jumping with his feet thrust forward so that he'd land on his back on the slope.

Ethan did the same, kicking his legs forward at the edge. He heard the crack of a bullet behind him and then he was over the side. Ethan's stomach lurched during a frozen moment of terror when he thought Jeff had made a bad error and that the drop they'd have to complete was measured in hundreds of feet and not just feet. Then he hit the slope on his back and slid.

He looked down to see Jeff several yards below him, then realized that his colleague had come to a halt, but it was too late for Ethan to stop himself and he slammed into him. The two men rolled over each other, each grabbing hold of the other before they came to a scrambling halt.

Ethan flopped back, realizing they were lying on a ledge. It was boulder-strewn and provided plenty of cover, but that cover wouldn't keep them safe for long.

'What now?' Ethan asked.

Jeff didn't reply. Instead, he hurried along the ledge towards the first of the two bodies that had come to rest here earlier. Above them, Ethan heard Duggan shouting orders to the other men. Within moments they would reach the edge and look down at them. Ethan saw what Jeff was aiming to do and he moved after him, shaking his head. He was about to express the futility of the attempt, but Jeff looked at him with a forlorn expression that said he knew this was a potentially hopeless plan, but they could do nothing else. Ethan agreed with this attitude and he hurried on to the second body.

By the time he'd reached it, Jeff had already tipped the first body over the side. Ethan matched his action, looping a foot under the man's chest then sending him spinning down the slope. Then he followed Jeff in hurrying for cover.

'Good try,' he whispered as he joined Jeff in lying flat behind a low boulder, 'but they had different clothing from ours and — '

'And they'll kick up plenty of dust. Now just keep down.'

This time Ethan did as ordered and kept his head down.

'Where are — ?' Duggan shouted from above.

'The fools,' someone else said.

'That's only one of them.'

'No. Look. The other's further down.'

Duggan snorted. 'I guess that saves us having to kill them. You two, find a way down there and check they're dead.'

'That fall just has to — '

'Just get down there and check.'

Ethan braced himself for discovery when the men climbed down and passed by their hiding place, but when two minutes had passed without them appearing he accepted that they'd taken a longer, and safer, route down.

'Well, Jeff,' he said, 'that damn fool plan worked, after all.'

'Don't get too pleased. We're still stuck here on this ledge, without guns, without — '

'This ain't the time for your self-pity. I'm just pleased we're still alive.' Ethan risked glancing up and confirmed nobody was looking over the edge. 'But we'll have to get away before those men find out the truth.'

Jeff agreed. They edged their way along the ledge, moving away from Lansford's grave and gradually reaching higher ground. They were several hundred yards along the ledge when a low cry from down below sounded. They couldn't hear the words, but it was undoubtedly confirmation that the men had found the bodies.

By then Ethan and Jeff had gained the sanctuary of a high point surrounded on all sides by rocks that guarded them from being seen from the pass. But the ledge had petered away to nothing and they could go no further forward. They agreed that heading up to the plateau above the pass would highlight them against the skyline. So they settled down to let the gathering darkness shroud them and aid the final part of their escape.

They found an overhanging stretch of rock and crawled beneath it. Then they could do nothing but wait and hope. Aside from occasionally hearing Duggan and his group moving around in the pass, they heard nothing to suggest their pursuers were coming close to them.

Gradually darkness fell, each drop in light-level improving their mood and making them feel safer. Only when full darkness had descended did they decide to move on.

Moving carefully in the darkness, they made their way out of the hollow and to the plateau. They heard no further noises from Duggan and his group, suggesting they'd remained in the pass, but as they moved across the plateau with only starlight to guide them their progress was slow.

They knew the plateau was wide and that the route they'd taken to come up to it would be navigable even in the dark, but they found it hard to judge where the edge of the plateau was. Both men felt constantly as if they were one step away from death. After several false alarms when they stumbled over small mounds, Jeff reported that the moon was due to rise in an hour, so Ethan readily agreed to wait for an increase in light-level.

Most of that hour had passed before Ethan dared to broach the subject that concerned him the most now that it appeared they'd escaped.

'What did Duggan mean about you not being trustworthy?' he asked.

Ethan heard a sharp intake of breath and Jeff didn't reply for several seconds.

'The two of us didn't exactly get on, as you know.'

Ethan wondered whether he should press the matter. He was sure there was something more behind Jeff's guarded answer, but after having saved his life, Jeff was certainly someone he could trust and he didn't want to offend him by probing at a matter that could be personal.

'I get the feeling,' he said, searching for a balance between prying and being supportive, 'that you weren't entirely honest with me about your reasons for coming with me. Perhaps you do have a personal grudge to settle with Duggan, after all?'

Jeff didn't reply immediately and when he did his voice had an emotional edge to it that Ethan couldn't fathom.

'Something like that.'

This time Ethan accepted that Jeff didn't want to talk about whatever problem he had with Duggan and he stood and stretched, looking around. Over to the west a faint glow was highlighting the ridge.

'Moon's coming up.'

Jeff sighed with what Ethan took to be relief now that he'd changed the subject, then coughed and when he spoke his voice had intrigue in the tone.

'Or is it?'

'What you mean?'

Jeff stood, joining Ethan in peering at the glow.

'Duggan came back to take us on and he implied it was because he'd gathered reinforcements, but perhaps that wasn't the reason. Perhaps he came back because the place where we found him was the place where he wanted to be.'

'The waiting place to get into Ansel Stark's hideout that Miguel spoke about?'

'Yeah.'

'That's intriguing, but if it's as secure

as Miguel said it was, even when the moon comes up, I doubt we'll be able to find it.'

'Except that isn't the moon over there. It'll still be below the horizon.' Jeff patted Ethan's back. 'I reckon it's a camp-fire, a heavily guarded camp-fire.'

'In a heavily guarded stronghold,' Ethan said.

9

Although Ethan and Jeff confirmed that the source of the light that they could see was a fire and not the moon, it still took them an hour to get close enough to look down into Ansel Stark's stronghold. By then the moon had risen and the light slipping through the low scudding cloud was strong enough to let them see that the stronghold was as well-hidden as Miguel had claimed it to be.

The area was a deep bowl, bounded on all sides by ridges that were several hundred feet high. When they'd made their way down into the bowl for a few dozen paces they saw that ten rough huts had been built at the bottom, protected from view unless someone happened to be standing directly above them. They couldn't see anyone moving around although the presence of the low fire meant people were here.

They readily agreed that attempting to get even closer to the huts in the dark when they couldn't discern the lie of the land was a bad idea. So they settled down to sleep and await the new day.

First light brought their first sighting of the position in which they'd rested. They were on a large flat boulder, about a third of the way down to the bottom of the bowl and so around 300 feet above the ground.

Unfortunately, above them was a distinct lack of cover all the way to the high ridges. So they agreed that the safest option would be to stay lying on the boulder for the rest of the day. This would let them gauge who was in the stronghold, but as they hadn't eaten or drunk since yesterday it was an activity neither man viewed with enthusiasm.

The sky was bright when they saw the first person. This proved to be a woman who emerged from a hut to bank up the fire from a store of wood before returning to the hut. An hour later two more people emerged and pottered around. From high up, and with neither man daring to keep themselves potentially exposed to view for long, they couldn't tell what they were doing, although they presumed they were preparing food.

Curiously, both these people were women too.

'Ansel Stark hasn't just got himself a stronghold up here,' Jeff said, 'he's set himself up with a community.'

Ethan nodded. 'I'm also getting the feeling he isn't here. And that means we've wasted our time finding this place.'

Jeff agreed with a sorry shake of the head. Then the two men settled down, trying to avoid being seen from below, but they need not have worried about trouble from that direction. They'd only been lying quietly for another hour, and the sun had yet to reach them, when Ethan heard an ominous click behind him, the sound coming from some distance away, but sounding like a rifle being locked. He swirled round on his belly to look behind him, a spontaneous gesture making him reach for a gun that wasn't there, but then he flinched away when a slug gouged a furrow into the rock beside his hand.

'Keep that hand where I can see it,' a woman shouted down at him, 'or the next shot will rip you in two.'

'We don't want no trouble,' Ethan shouted back, playing for time. 'We were aiming to leave.'

'Nobody leaves here.'

Further up the slope a woman stood and as Ethan sized her up, wondering whether he could rush her, two more women stood and paced into view to form a line on the edge of the ridge. They were all armed, barefoot, hard-boned and dressed in crudely constructed clothes. With firm hand gestures they signified that Ethan and Jeff should rise and put their hands on their heads. Then they headed down towards them. With-out further comment they signified that they should precede them down to ground level.

The route down was steep, but with the women's aid in pointing out a narrow trail they reached ground level in a few minutes. Once there, around a dozen womenfolk emerged from the huts to consider them.

The woman who had fired at Ethan spoke to the other women, checking that they hadn't seen any other men. On hearing their negative responses Ethan learned that the woman who had shot at them was called Nora.

'What you come here for?' she asked, her rifle still aimed at Ethan.

'We're friends of Duggan Ward,' Ethan said, keeping a straight face.

'That don't answer my question.'

'And we have important information for Ansel Stark.'

'Which is?'

'It's for his ears only, not for his woman.'

Nora bristled with indignation as Ethan's guess apparently proved correct. While she regained her composure she darted her gaze towards a blonde woman. This woman was young, fresh-faced and from her dignified stance somewhat out of place amongst this group.

'You all know you can't come in,' she said, her voice lighter than Nora's, but just as commanding, 'until Ansel invites you in.'

Ethan breathed a sigh of relief at the apparent acceptance of their story that they knew Ansel Stark.

'Then ask him. I'm sure he won't mind that we got here early.'

Nora sneered at the unlikelihood of this being true.

'Like she said, his orders never change and you've made a fatal mistake.' Nora raised the rifle to sight Ethan while the other two armed women turned their weapons on Jeff.

Ethan had no doubt these women would kill them and he darted his gaze around the other women, hoping to catch someone's eye and see a hint of compassion. Only one woman was looking at him with anything less than contempt, and this was the blonde woman. She was also familiar . . .

'Wait!' Ethan said. He fixed this woman with his gaze. 'That isn't our whole story. We're also friends of Lansford.'

'Never heard of him,' Nora snorted, but Ethan wasn't interested in her reaction. He looked at the blonde woman and received the reaction he'd hoped for. She flinched back a pace, a hand darting up to her mouth, her legs buckling before she got herself under control.

'Don't kill them,' she said, stepping forward.

Nora turned her contemptuous gaze on her.

'And why is this Lansford important to Ansel?'

'I don't know. I've never heard of anyone with that name. I just reckon you shouldn't kill them in case they are telling the truth and they do have information for Ansel.'

'Just because you have Ansel's ear these days, it doesn't mean he doesn't still trust my judgement.'

The woman paced up to Nora and considered her with cold contempt.

'I have more than Ansel's ear these days, as you well know, but you're right. Sometimes he does trust the *older* members.'

The emphasis in her comment along with Nora's firm jaw hinted at the power struggle that had existed within this group long before they'd arrived and the result of that struggle was one on which their lives depended. For long moments the two women fixed each other with their firm gazes until to Ethan's relief Nora was the first to look away.

'All right,' she said, 'put them in the cage.'

Nora then snapped orders to the other armed women to deal with their incarceration, implying that she hadn't backed down and taken another person's orders but that it was her will all along that they should live. Following her directions, they headed away from the huts and towards the slope.

As Ethan looked ahead to see where their prison would be while they awaited Ansel's return Jeff shuffled closer, looking for an opportunity to ask the question that so obviously burned on his mind. They had been directed to climb back up the slope before he got that chance.

'Who was that woman who saved us?' he asked. 'You seemed to know her.'

'Never met her before,' Ethan said, 'but I saw her picture in a locket yesterday. She's Mary, Mary Donner.'

* * *

The cell in which Sheriff Fisher had held Ethan was typical of the cells in which he had been incarcerated on the rare occasions when he'd got himself into trouble with the law. Despite his lack of experience with such confined spaces he reckoned there couldn't be a worse cell in which to be imprisoned.

Nora directed them to get into a wooden cage that was barely big enough for the two of them, being only six feet high and five feet wide. It sat on a protruding ledge 200 feet above ground level, providing them with a vertigo-inducing view of the huts below.

Worse was to follow.

Beside the cage was a crane and pulley system, which Ethan assumed they used to lower horses and supplies down to ground level. This time they used it for a far more disconcerting manoeuvre. They attached a rope to the cage, winched it off the ground, then swung it out over the 200 foot drop.

The wooden structure creaked and swayed as if it might collapse at any moment and both men hung on to the sides, not daring to move in case they broke the loosely lashed wooden bars beneath their feet. Neither man dared to look down even when the cage came to a swaying halt twenty feet out from the ledge.

'Enjoy your wait for Ansel,' Nora said behind them.

Ethan looked back and saw her smirk, his action setting the cage to swaying then turning in a creaking slow movement that sent nauseous bile rising in his throat.

The equally green-looking Jeff also gulped.

'We need to sit,' he said, 'and then not move an inch.'

Ethan acknowledged that standing in the top-heavy cage was the worst thing they could do and so, in a co-ordinated move, both men sat opposite each other. Thankfully this reduced the swaying and when the slow turning of the cage had stopped so did the continual creaking.

Then there was nothing for either of them to do other than to try to avoid moving too much, and to try to avoid looking downwards at the people milling around below.

'I never thought I'd say this,' Ethan said by way of something to talk about and to take his mind off their predicament, 'but I now feel real sorry for Lansford.'

'Because he was so close to finding his wife, yet died just a mile or so away from her?'

'Yeah. And he spent years destroying himself thinking she was dead, and she was alive all along.'

Jeff shrugged. 'Maybe if he'd known she was alive it might have torn him up even worse. It sounds as if Mary has had to . . . to ingratiate herself with Ansel Stark to stay alive.'

'She may have been forced to warm his bed, but she had the courage to speak up for us. Ansel hasn't destroyed the woman Lansford remembered.'

'But can she help us when we're stuck up here?'

Ethan gave a forlorn shrug after which their conversation petered out and they settled in to wait out the day while moving as little as possible. Despite their uncomfortable positions the exertions of the last day meant that both men managed to doze, and so it was with a start that Ethan awoke when he heard someone speaking nearby. He snapped round to look at the ledge, seeing that Mary was looking at them. Unfortunately, his sudden movement set the cage to swinging.

'Can you help us?' Ethan asked when he'd confirmed she was alone.

'Perhaps,' she said, 'but don't talk so loudly and take this before anyone watching gets suspicious.'

Ethan noted she was holding a pole with a ladle on the end towards them. They avoided moving until she'd managed to poke the ladle through a gap in the bars. While the grateful Jeff slurped down the water in the ladle Ethan spoke to her.

'I'm right and you are Mary Donner, aren't you?'

'I am,' she said.

'Lansford was right about you. You're a right — '

'Don't waste time on flattery,' she said, withdrawing the ladle now that Jeff had drained it. 'Where is he?'

Before he'd dozed Ethan had pondered on what he would say to her if he got the chance, and as he hated having to lie, he chose his words carefully.

'He's close.' He gestured beyond the ridge. 'A mile or so over there.'

Jeff shot him a shocked glance, which Ethan ignored and which Mary didn't see as she refilled the ladle.

'That's good to hear,' she said as she started handing the pole out again. 'How is he?'

Ethan couldn't answer that in a truthful manner without revealing something he didn't want to do and so he stretched a hand through the bars while licking his lips as if he was desperate for the water. He caught hold of the ladle and drew it in then sipped down the water while thinking quickly. No idea would come to him, but luckily Mary didn't wait for a reply.

'I take it,' she said, 'from your silence that he didn't take my kidnapping well?'

'It was hard on him,' Ethan said,

pausing from his drinking. 'But he never gave up hope these last two years.'

'I knew he wouldn't. That's why I . . . I did whatever I had to do to survive.'

'I'm sure nobody would blame you.' Ethan offered a smile that she returned, her relief speaking of the fact that her main concern was still how Lansford would react to the news of how she'd survived. 'But if we're ever to get away, we need your help.'

She nodded. 'I'll do that, but when will Lansford come?'

Ethan gritted his teeth as beside him Jeff murmured to himself under his breath, but Ethan had committed himself to this course of action and he couldn't veer away now.

'I don't know.'

'But didn't he send you on ahead?'

'It wasn't like that,' he said, speaking quickly to convey the urgency of the situation and, he hoped, turn her away from this line of questioning and on to how they would escape. 'We joined up with him because we all had different reasons to get Ansel Stark. But we couldn't find this stronghold so we split up. Lansford isn't far away, but he might not get in here.'

Jeff grumbled as Ethan's explanations went beyond evading the truth, but Mary was now fidgeting and not paying attention to him as she looked down into the stronghold. She raised a hand.

'Enough talk,' she said. 'People are starting to look up here. I won't be able to feed you again today or that'll raise suspicions, but I'll come tonight, long after dark when everyone is asleep.'

She gestured up at the crane holding them to the ridge, suggesting their future escape route. Then she turned on her heel and made her way down to the huts.

'So we just have to last out for the rest of the day,' Ethan said. He looked at Jeff, who was shaking his head.

'That was wrong, Ethan,' he said. 'You should have told her.'

'I didn't want to destroy her in here after everything she's been through. I'll tell her the full story later.'

Jeff narrowed his eyes. 'And is that the real reason?'

Ethan acknowledged Jeff's scepticism with a shrug.

'Partly. I can't deny I was also worried she'd fall apart and might not help us.'

'She appears to be a strong and decent woman. No matter what your reasoning, you didn't have the right to let her think we'd lead her to her husband when the best we can do is to lead her to his grave.'

Ethan searched for the right words to argue his case, but he couldn't find them. He lowered his head, and so, with the disapproving Jeff sitting in the cramped cell before him, their first day of captivity passed slowly.

Twice during the afternoon women arrived to pass out water to them. Neither of them was Mary. Later, when the sun had drifted away from the stronghold another woman arrived with a small bowl of stale bread and tough, rank-smelling meat.

By the time they'd eaten Ethan had overcome his vertigo sufficiently to look down at the ground. He saw Mary moving around helping with the preparation of dinner and the stoking of the fire for the night. He also noted that she was giving Nora a wide berth.

Other than when they moved positions to ease the cramps he and Jeff shared few words. Despite the shame Ethan felt for his actions, as night fell his spirits rose somewhat and he offered Jeff a shamefaced sigh.

'All right,' he said, 'I'll admit you were right. I should have told her the truth and trusted that she'd still help us.'

Jeff nodded. 'Glad you said that, but I reckon you'll be the one who'll regret your decision the most when you have to tell her that truth.'

Ethan offered a rueful smile in acknowledgement of this sentiment then returned to watching what was happening below. Presently the women retired to their huts. Silence descended with the gathering darkness. The low moon didn't light the whole of the crucible, but the fire let them see enough to make out the huts and anyone who happened to move around.

Ethan had expected Mary to wait until the middle of the night before she made her move, but he saw a figure emerge several hours after everyone had retired. She looked up at them and made a gesture before her face, which Ethan took to be her calling for silence. Then she made her way over to the side of the slope and clambered up it.

Earlier three women had strained to move the cage over the side, so Ethan couldn't see how she'd planned to do the task on her own. But as she approached he saw that she'd slung a coil of rope over her shoulder.

'Seems as we're going to have to make a jump for it,' Ethan said.

'The only thing worse than being in a

cage,' Jeff murmured unhappily, 'is jumping out of one.'

By the time she'd arrived on the ledge both men had agreed how they would make the tricky manoeuvre. Although Ethan couldn't convince Jeff that it'd be safe, he instructed her to make a loop, then lasso the pulley above the cage. Then they would have to break through the cage, grab the rope, and swing out on to the ledge.

Luckily her plans were also broadly of the same nature and she'd brought a knife with which to cut through the ropes that secured the cage door. She placed the knife in the ladle then began to hand it out across the gap towards them. But then she flinched and stopped.

'What's wrong?' Ethan demanded.

She didn't reply, instead standing with her head to one side, listening. She murmured a strangulated sob of despair a moment before a loud cry went up from the ridge to their side. The person hollered so loudly his voice echoed back and forth in the cauldron several times.

'I'm back!'

Ethan and Jeff shot each other a worried glance, but it was Mary who provided the answer.

'Ansel Stark,' she whispered.

'Then you have to get us out of here now,' Ethan urged.

'I do,' she murmured, backing away from the edge.

'Then do it. Throw me the knife. Throw the rope over the pulley.' He waited, but she continued to back away. 'Just do it. Do it now.'

'I have to go,' she said, shaking her head. 'I'm sorry. I'll do what I can to make sure he doesn't kill you, but I have to look after myself first. Lansford is near and he'll find me soon. I've survived for him this long. I have to continue doing whatever I have to do to survive for his sake.'

With that comment she kicked the rope and knife over to the side of the ledge and out of view then headed away.

Ethan urged her to help one last time as loudly as he dared then sank back down to the bottom of the cage in forlorn acceptance of the fact that she wasn't going to risk helping them after all. Beside him Jeff thankfully kept his silence.

'You don't need to say it,' Ethan murmured as Mary reached ground level unnoticed. 'I should have told her the truth. Then she'd have had nothing to lose and might still have helped us.'

'You should,' Jeff said simply. Then he shuffled round to look down at the ground and watch the womenfolk emerge to welcome in the returning men.

Ethan soon picked out the form of Ansel Stark leading a line of around twenty men downwards. Most of these were blindfolded and so were having difficulty picking a path, but Ethan's gaze centred on one man. Ansel was leading this man and when they were near ground level he reached back to remove his blindfold. That man rubbed at his face, then put a hand to his brow and with uncanny luck his gaze centred in on the cage. From several hundred feet away Ethan couldn't see his face, but he could imagine that Duggan Ward was smiling.

Then the group headed down to the huts, and for the next half-hour pandemonium reigned. Nobody paid them any attention.

Celebratory gunfire exploded into the air, mercifully none of it coming close to the cage. Liquor appeared and flowed. The sounds of revelry from around the fire filled the cauldron.

Ethan noted that Mary let Ansel paw her. All the time Nora hovered nearby, her frequent glances at the cage signifying she was waiting for the right time to mention their presence in a way that would earn Ansel's favour and lose Mary some of hers.

Eventually she got his attention and a small group of Ansel, Mary, Nora and Duggan made their way up to a low ledge to consider them. They were several hundred feet away so, aside from catching the occasional word, Ethan couldn't hear their conversation, but from their tone and body language he was able to judge the conversation that then took place.

Ansel demanded to know who they were and why they were in the cage.

Mary explained that she was unsure why they'd come here and so she'd thought it best to keep them there until he'd returned.

With much relish Nora reported that she had thought killing them straight away would have been the right thing to do.

Ansel shrugged and replied that he was more interested in returning to the revelry than considering them. He turned to go, but Duggan stood before him. He stated that Nora's plan was the right one and that they should resolve Mary's mistake immediately by killing them.

Ansel quizzed him as to why he was so eager to see these men dead.

Duggan briefly explained their history. Ethan noted Mary's reactions, but she didn't respond so Duggan couldn't have mentioned Lansford's death. Before he'd finished Ansel waved a dismissive hand that pleased Nora and Duggan, suggesting he'd agreed to dispose of them straight away, but Mary swung round to stand before him and whispered something in his ear. This made Nora and Duggan shoot irritated glances at each other until Ansel laughed, then walked away, nodding.

Duggan objected to Ansel's decision, demanding to know why he'd made it. This made Ansel stop and glare at him, angry now. He barked a demand.

'Because I enjoy it,' he said, his loud and cryptic comment reaching them.

This didn't pacify Duggan who continued to glower, but Nora relaxed somewhat and hurried off ahead down to ground level, followed by Ansel and Mary, and last of all Duggan.

'She saved us,' Jeff said, sighing with relief.

Ethan was about to agree, but then he saw Mary look up at them. Even from such a distance he could see the anguish on her face and he saw her mouth something to them. He couldn't be sure what she'd said, but he thought he understood.

'I'm sorry,' Ethan murmured.

'What?' Jeff said.

'That's what she just said. She's sorry, but about what? She's just saved our . . . ' Ethan trailed off, the terrible answer coming to him. There are fates worse than sudden, violent death, and he had a feeling they would soon suffer one of those fates.

But if Ansel had a painful scheme in store for them, he made them wait for it. When the group returned to ground level he barked out orders and so forced some level of organization on to the riotous activities below.

The men set out a table on which they placed jars of liquor. Most of the women disentangled themselves from the men, formed a circle, and set about performing an activity that Ethan couldn't discern, but which involved cutting a rope into short lengths and collecting small rocks.

Ansel gestured to a hut and two men went in to emerge with two women in tow. These women were tied up. Ethan hadn't seen either of them before, so presumably they were also being held prisoner. They were stood before Ansel who paraded before them, his frequent glances at Duggan suggesting his posturing was also directed at him. One woman kept her head bowed but the other woman stared defiantly at Ansel, then jerked her head forward.

Ansel rubbed his cheek, suggesting she'd spat at him and, in anger, he slapped her face knocking her to her knees.

Beside him Jeff drew in his breath, an alarmed bleat of anguish slipping from his lips as he showed far greater concern than Ansel's minor burst of savagery should have warranted. Ethan shot him a glance, but Jeff didn't look at him. Instead, he pressed his face to the bottom of the cage to peer intently at the events below, his eyes transfixed and his mouth open in a display of shock.

Ethan returned his gaze to the bottom to see Ansel gesturing towards the fire then to the standing woman. A man stepped forward, grabbed the woman's arms from behind and forced her towards the fire.

'No!' the woman on the ground cried, making Ethan steel himself for what he thought would happen next. Sure enough the man stopped before the fire and held the woman towards it in a gesture that held an obvious threat.

'Do it!' Ansel shouted. 'Or she dies.'

Ansel glared down at the prostrate woman, who threw her bound hands before her face. Everyone stood watching the frozen tableau, looking at the woman by the fire then to Ansel and the other woman.

'What does he want her to do?' Jeff murmured.

The answer came when the woman's shoulders slumped in a show of compliance. She stood, batted the dust from her clothing, and raised her arms. Then she began singing. Her clear, angelic voice drifted up to them, and in any other situation it would have made Ethan's heart soar.

The first notes made Ansel holster his gun. Then everyone gathered round to listen to her sing in awed silence and with greater reverence than Ethan would have thought them capable of showing. They sat cross-legged around her as her pure voice quelled everyone's former revelry. Beyond the circle the women working on the rope swayed from side to side letting the song aid them in their task.

'That wasn't as bad as I expected,' Ethan said with relief. 'I just hope Ansel saves us if we sing, although I couldn't sing that well.'

He laughed but when Jeff didn't respond to his grim attempt at humour he looked at him. Jeff was still lying with his face pressed to the bottom of the cage, staring at the people below.

'What's wrong?' Ethan asked. When he didn't get an answer he tapped Jeff's shoulder. The action made Jeff flinch away, then sit hunched in the corner of the cage.

'I know that woman,' he said simply, not meeting Ethan's eye as his motion sent the cage to rocking. 'She's Lavinia Clancy. The older woman is her sister.'

'The women from Bluff Point?'

'Yeah.'

'Then that's good news.'

'It isn't,' Jeff whined, burying his head in his hands. 'If they're being held captive here along with Mary Donner, it means Ansel Stark was behind the massacre at Bluff Point, after all.'

'But we knew that,' Ethan said, bemused. He waited for Jeff to explain himself but he'd drawn his legs up to his chin and was rocking back and forth, having retreated into himself. 'You'll have to explain what you mean.'

'I can't,' Jeff murmured eventually,

not meeting Ethan's eye. 'Ansel Stark massacred the Clancy family at Bluff Point. He did it. He did it.'

'He did,' Ethan said, furrowing his brow and trying to put understanding into his voice despite his confusion, 'just like he wiped out Sam Pringle's outfit.'

Jeff swallowed then looked up at Ethan. Tears glistened in his eyes.

'Ansel killed the Clancy family, but he didn't . . . he didn't . . . ' His voice trailed off. He coughed to clear his throat before he continued. 'Ansel didn't kill Sam Pringle.'

'Then who did?' Ethan asked.

'I did,' Jeff said.

10

'Jeff,' Ethan said, shaking his head in bemusement, 'I know you've got into the habit of blaming yourself for everything that's happened to us, but you saved my life back in Bluff Point. I can't see how you can think yourself responsible.'

'Because I am,' Jeff murmured, lowering his head. 'I led Sam Pringle's outfit to the bluff and they got killed. It's my fault.'

Ethan considered his unhappy companion. Ever since they'd left Bluff Point, Jeff had involved himself in Ethan's problems. Although he'd accepted that it was out of friendship, he'd never been able to shake the feeling that there was something Jeff didn't want to tell him.

He patted Jeff's shoulder to get his attention then encouraged him to raise his head and fixed him with his firm gaze.

'Jeff, just take a deep breath and tell me everything — and this time the full truth.'

Jeff did as requested, taking a long calming breath. When he spoke up, his voice was low and serious. His eyes stayed downcast.

'Everything I told you about what happened at Bluff Point was the truth, except I left out . . . ' Jeff rubbed his forehead. 'Like I said, Rory and Isaac rode into town and harassed Lavinia Clancy in the saloon. They thought she was a saloon girl but she wasn't and they wouldn't take no for an answer, if you know what I mean.'

'I do. Go on.'

'They were drunk and determined to cause trouble. Duggan Ward got into an argument with them, then helped throw them out of the saloon. They vowed to get even and I guess now I know it was just talk, but they hung around town that night, and someone claimed he saw them follow Lavinia when she left town to go home. When the whole family turned up dead the next day, everyone was angry.'

Ethan nodded, sensing an inkling of what Jeff was trying to tell him.

'Then Sheriff Fisher should have come out to the outfit and questioned Rory and Isaac.'

'He should have, but I now reckon he suspected the truth. Ansel killed them as a warning to Duggan as to what would happen if he didn't help him with the bank raid. Duggan couldn't let this become known and so he demanded revenge against two convenient scapegoats, saying a court would never prove anything.' Jeff looked up and met his eye, that gaze pleading. 'I agreed to help them. I came out, pretending I was looking for work, but I just came to draw the outfit to the bluff where — '

'You did what?' Ethan snapped.

'I . . . I . . . I did it. I led the outfit into an ambush and got everyone killed.

But you got to believe this — I never expected that to happen.'

'Then what was supposed to happen?'

'Duggan had organized a group of men to do the job.' Jeff gestured down to the people milling below, who were still listening to Lavinia sing. 'Some of those men, I guess. They were to surround the outfit, isolate Rory and Isaac, then take them away for questioning.'

'And a lynching?'

Jeff looked away. 'I suppose that's what would have happened, but I didn't worry too much about their fate. I'd seen the bodies and I was just as angry as everyone else was. But then the shooting started and I suppose the men Duggan hired just weren't interested in taking prisoners.'

'And ever since then you've lied to me.'

'I didn't know what I should do. I tried to make amends. I tried to help you find Ansel. I spoke up for you at your trial. I came with you to find Duggan — '

'Obliged,' Ethan grunted, sarcastically.

'I deserve that. You're right. I didn't come to help you, but to ease my conscience. I'd hoped we could find Duggan and prove he was guilty of helping Ansel, but innocent of the murder of the Clancy family. At least then I might find some justification for getting Sam Pringle and everyone else killed, but I was wrong . . . ' Jeff trailed off, unable to continue.

Ethan searched for the words to respond to someone whom he'd thought of as a friend but who he now knew had perpetrated the worst betrayal of all. He couldn't find those words and the longer the silence went on, the more he found he had nothing to say on the matter.

Instead, he looked down on the proceedings below where Lavinia had now stopped singing. The men were standing around the circle of women. Several men were hefting the short ropes the women had made and to

avoid thinking of Jeff and his treacherous activities he watched them, trying
to work out what they were doing.

Only when they started moving
towards the ledge did he realize what
was about to happen. He turned to Jeff.

'And what punishment do you expect
for your actions?'

'I deserve to die,' Jeff said.

Ethan flashed him a grim smile.
'Then you're about to get that wish.'

He didn't explain further but turned
to look at the group of men who were
now standing on the ledge facing the
cage. They were holding the lengths of
rope, each of which had small rocks
tied to their ends. Several men were
gesturing with wads of bills as bets were
laid. Then they started on the night's
entertainment.

Jeff asked several times what they
were doing, but Ethan ignored him,
leaving him to find out in due course.

The first man stepped forward with a
short rope dangling from his hand. He
drew back his arm, whirled the rope

over his head, the rocks spinning the rope to tremendous velocity, then released it. The missile swirled off across the gap heading straight for the cage, but it didn't have enough momentum and dropped before it reached them, then crashed to the ground below. A chorus of catcalls arose from the watching audience.

'They're going to stone us to death,' Jeff murmured.

'That's their plan,' Ethan said, 'and their sport.'

He watched the second man step up. He was burlier than the first man and his throw flew from his hand with far greater strength. It headed straight for the cage. Both men tensed then flinched away as it crashed into the bars, cracking one before it tumbled away.

'The bars saved us,' Jeff said with relief when the cage had stopped swaying from the impact.

Ethan fingered the broken bar, judging that a second blow would break it.

'This time it did. As far as I can see, we either get stoned to death, or they break enough of the bars so that we fall to our deaths.'

Jeff winced as the next man took up his position.

'I wish there was some way I could take this punishment instead of you.'

'Save it. I don't want to die listening to your whining.' Ethan then dismissed Jeff from his thoughts and put his attention into trying to avoid the whirling rocks.

The next one smashed into the underside of the cage, setting the cage to shaking and again cracking through a bar. Ethan stepped back to avoid putting his weight on that bar, only to find the next rock smashing into the wall above his head, making him duck down.

The next rock hit the bottom again, this time breaking the entire bar and making it fall away to leave a gaping hole in the middle of the cage.

'Looks as if you won't have to die

listening to me whining for long,' Jeff said, peering down through the hole.

As it was the cage withstood far more damage than Ethan expected. The men's tiring arms along with their increasingly drink-fuelled poor aim meant that at least half the rocks didn't hit the cage and those that did only cracked bars. Each bar needed at least two hits before it broke.

But gradually the damage started to threaten the structure and Ethan and Jeff had to tread carefully around the growing holes in the cage.

Ethan couldn't help but peer through those holes, wondering whether he should end the torment by just dropping through, but he clung on to the hope that Mary would step in and help them. She was staying close to Ansel, talking to him, he hoped, encouraging him to end the game, but he showed no sign of doing this. In fact as the cage became more fragile the competition amongst his men grew fiercer as to who would be the one to make them fall to their deaths.

The first inkling that they might get a reprieve came from an unlikely source.

Ethan noticed that the competition was entirely amongst a small group of men and that the people who weren't participating had gathered around Duggan Ward beside the huts. Ethan couldn't be sure but he reckoned those men were the ones who had been with Duggan back in the pass. Duggan spent several minutes speaking to them. Then they parted and one at a time made their way up on to the ledge. They kept in the shadows and out of the way of the competitors as they took up positions at the back of the ledge.

When they'd reached the ledge Duggan joined them and faced the backs of Ansel and the other men.

His attempt to seize control was sudden and effective.

Ansel's men were all concentrating on the competition and so didn't see Duggan give a quick gesture. As one, his men drew their guns and fired into the competitors' backs. At least six men went down in the initial onslaught, the men tumbling forward over the ledge to fall to the ground below. Others took several seconds to comprehend the sudden change in their circumstances from the excitement of the approaching end of their game to their outright slaughter.

Duggan's men made them pay for their slowness with another deadly round of gunfire. Only a few survived to fight back and these took out at least two men apiece, but, as they stood exposed on the edge of the ledge one by one Duggan's men picked them off.

Ansel was amongst the survivors and he organized a retreat down from the ledge. Along with three other men and Nora he attempted to reach a hut to mount a defence. They never reached it. A volley of gunfire cut through the retreating group before they'd halved the distance to the hut. The gunfire left only Ansel standing. He stopped and turned to look up at Duggan, his hunched stance reflecting the truth that he had only survived because Duggan had wanted him to.

'Get down here, you yellow-belly,' Ansel shouted.

Duggan shouted a taunt that made Ansel grunt with anger, then fire at him, but a returning gunshot winged his gun from his hand.

Then Duggan made his way down to the ground level to face him. Despite his successful takeover, Ansel's men had decimated Duggan's ranks, only three men surviving to follow him down. Aside from Mary, the women had fled to the relative safety of the huts.

'Let's hope,' Jeff said in the cage, 'Duggan's forgotten about us.'

'No hope of that,' Ethan murmured, half-expecting what was about to follow.

Sure enough, Duggan ordered a man to secure Ansel. While that man took his arms from behind and pushed him towards the slope, Duggan moved over to Mary. He cast a glance at the hut into which Lavinia had fled then grabbed her arm. She struggled at first but then relented when she saw that none of the other women would come to their aid, and with the air of a man who'd claimed his trophy Duggan walked behind Ansel.

The group made their way upwards towards the ledge before the cage. When they arrived, Duggan directed two men to swing the cage back towards the ledge.

'What you reckon he's going to do?' Jeff whispered from the corner of his mouth.

Ethan ignored him, finding that if these were to be his last few moments he'd prefer to spend them planning a potentially futile assault against Duggan rather than listen to his former friend. Duggan must have been aware of the possibility that Ethan might try something because when the cage slapped down on to the ledge he ordered one man to stand before him. Another man moved in and swung the door open.

With his gun Duggan gestured for Jeff to get out. Jeff shot Ethan a glance before he moved, but again Ethan ignored him, and so Jeff bowed his head and stepped out on to the ledge. He took a pace forward, then turned.

'I just want you to know,' he said, 'that I'm sorry.'

Ethan knew he ought to forgive him, but instead he shook his head.

'Go to hell, Jeff,' he said.

Then Ethan moved to follow him out, but Duggan grunted a demand that he stay where he was. He ordered the man holding Ansel to push him into the cage beside Ethan and then without closing the door, the other two men used the crane to swing the cage back out from the ledge.

In the cage Ethan looked at Ansel, who returned a snarling glare that perhaps acknowledged that they'd met before. With much creaking the cage returned to its previous position, dangling 200 feet up and about twenty feet out from the ledge.

'What now?' Ansel grunted, returning his gaze on to Duggan.

Duggan licked his lips, relishing his response.

'Whichever one of you lives . . . gets to live.'

Ethan had no doubt this was an empty promise and he guessed that Ansel would know that too but with an angry grunt Ansel reacted immediately. He swung his fist back-handed, crashing it into Ethan's chest and sending him tumbling into the cage wall, which creaked. A bar snapped away but the rest held.

Ethan teetered, fighting to keep his balance and before he could regroup his senses Ansel was on him. Two large hands snapped around his neck and pushed him back into the wall aiming to force him against the loosened and cracked bars and make him break through.

Ethan felt a bar behind his back

bend, then snap, forcing him backwards another foot and making it impossible for him to brace his feet on the base of the cage. He heard shouting coming from the ledge. One of the voices was Jeff's and even Mary joined in, but whether they were shouting encouragement to him or confronting Duggan, Ethan couldn't tell.

In desperation he kicked out. His foot slammed into Ansel's shins, but without purchase on the cage floor he was unable to deliver much force behind the blow. He kicked again trying to loop his foot behind Ansel's ankle and topple him, but Ansel had planted his feet firmly. He tried jabbing his fists into Ansel's chest, but they were so close together the blows landed without much force and now the iron-like grip around his neck had cut off his breathing.

Motes of light and darkness appeared to dance around Ansel's flared eyes and reddening face. A roar was building in Ethan's ears, but not so loudly that he couldn't hear the bar behind him screech out in protest. His memory of the cage wall told him this bar was the only one stopping him from falling.

Then the bar snapped. The force reverberated down Ethan's spine as if it were his own bones that had snapped. He fell backwards. Nothing was behind him to stop him tumbling the 200 feet to the ground — except one thing. He lunged out and grabbed a firm grip of Ansel's shirt with one hand and his upper arm with the other. He stopped moving, angled backwards with his head protruding from the cage and only his grip of his assailant keeping him from falling.

He locked his gaze on Ansel's eyes and with his stern look alone conveyed the fact that he'd never release his grip and that if he fell, they both fell. Ansel squirmed and with his elbows splayed he managed to prise the hand on his shirt away, but that only let Ethan grab a firm grip of his arm.

Ansel perhaps could have waited

Ethan out as the darkness was growing around him and his limbs were becoming numb, but impatience got the better of him. With a grunt of annoyance Ansel released his grip of Ethan's throat, clamped both hands down on his shoulders, then dragged him back into the cage. He twisted as he threw him, aiming to step aside and hurl Ethan through a gap in the opposite corner of the cage, but Ethan kept his grip of Ansel's arms and also twisted, throwing himself at him.

Ansel teetered. Then both men went down. The repeated slamming of the rocks into the bars had severely weakened the structure. So, as Ethan fell he aimed for a complete length of bar, but even that cracked. A cacophony of grinding and tearing sounded around him as they sprawled entangled on the bottom of the cage. Then he plummeted.

He was vaguely aware of Ansel suffering the same fate as he too fell through the bottom of the cage, but

Ethan had no time to worry about him. The bottom of the stronghold loomed below him with nothing between him and the ground to break his fall. He lunged out, his frantic, flailing arms hitting broken bars until with a twist of the wrist he clawed a hand around a bar. He fell with the bar held above his head and for a terrible moment he thought the bar had become unattached, but then a sudden jerk brought him to a halt, dangling one-handed beneath the cage. He ventured a glance upwards to see he had grabbed hold of the end of a broken bar, that bar swinging loose and only connected to the base of the wall.

He breathed a sigh of relief but then a solid blow slammed into his knees, sending him swinging backwards, the bar creaking ominously above him. He just had time to realize that Ansel had also managed to grab hold of a broken bar beside him when another kick slammed into his thigh. The bar holding him creaked then slipped, plunging him down another foot, but mercifully taking him out of the range of Ansel's blows. This let him appraise his assailant's predicament and he saw that Ansel had fared better than himself.

He had both hands stuck straight upright holding onto a solid length of crossbeam. Ansel considered Ethan's position, then abandoned his attempts to dislodge him. He rocked back and forth. Then, with a flexing of his biceps he drew his knees up to his chest, kicked his legs above his head, then backwards. His momentum somersaulted him until he landed his body over the beam.

In other circumstances this manoeuvre would have impressed Ethan, but it was clear what Ansel would do next and that gave Ethan only a few seconds to save himself. He threw up his other hand and grabbed the bar above his head, then hauled himself upwards, aiming to reach the cage before Ansel could clamber over and dislodge the bar.

Ansel was still lying over the beam, looking at him upside down while he regained his breath for his next manoeuvre. This encouraged Ethan to be more reckless. He scrambled hand over hand, clawing his way up the bar until his head tapped into the beam Ansel was resting on.

Ansel grunted with irritation on seeing his quick movement then put his weight on the beam, aiming to lift himself off it. This was what Ethan had hoped he'd do. Ethan put his shoulder to the beam and yanked himself up. He couldn't deliver much force behind the movement but the cage bottom had been severely weakened. The beam snapped, then fell.

A cry slipped from Ansel's lips as the beam on which he'd put all his weight suddenly plummeted from him and he dropped. He clawed out a hand, grabbing a dangling bar, and for a moment the bar held, letting him swing free beside Ethan, but Ethan repaid him for his previous attempt to dislodge him. He kicked up both his feet, planted them against Ansel's shoulders and pushed. The blow was strong enough and with a final crack of timbers Ansel fell away from the cage, becoming smaller and smaller until he slammed to the ground.

Ethan didn't waste time on being relieved. Hand over hand he pulled himself up into the cage. Then, keeping his feet on the outside of the cage to minimize the strain he stood on the strongest-looking remnant of bar. Only when he was sure it would hold him did he look to the people on the ledge.

Mary put a hand to her chest in a show of relief, but Jeff was looking at him with dead eyes as if Ethan's rejection of his apology had driven all the fight from him. Duggan was smiling and, with a mocking sneer on his face, he clapped once.

'Well done, Ethan,' he said. 'Your desire to live is extraordinary.'

'And your promise?' Ethan prompted as the bar he was standing on creaked then shifted its position downwards in a disconcerting manner.

Duggan offered a cold smile. 'Did you really believe me?'

11

Duggan paced forward to the edge to face Ethan then gestured to his men, one of whom joined him. The other two dragged Mary and Jeff forward.

Ethan still couldn't bring himself to forgive Jeff for his actions, but, it being clear that Duggan was going to kill him within seconds, he felt the anger that had driven him on for the last few weeks recede. He looked at Jeff and caught his eye.

'We're fine,' he mouthed.

Jeff nodded, relief spreading across his face. Then, as if he'd noticed the terrible predicament they were in for the first time, he straightened up and snapped his head round to look at Duggan. Ethan reckoned he was searching for something he could do that would help him, an act that was surely doomed to fail, but Ethan envied him. He'd rather meet his end trying to kill Duggan than just standing precariously in a broken cage waiting to be shot.

Duggan was taking his time in acting, drinking in Ethan's hopeless situation and this gave Jeff time to act. But when he did, it was not in the way Ethan had thought he would. He edged closer to Mary, bent towards her, then whispered something in her ear.

Despite the desperate situation she still leaned towards him with interest, but then her mouth fell open and she shot Ethan a look that was both angry and glassy-eyed with despair.

Ethan gulped as the realization hit him. Jeff had told her the truth about Lansford.

She rocked back and forth, her distress growing. Then she squealed and tore herself away from the man holding her. With her hands held out like claws she charged at Duggan. Perhaps at heart Duggan was a decent man, or at least not a cold-blooded killer like Ansel Stark, because he hesitated and that gave her enough time to barge into him. They went down with him trying to defend himself while she clawed and scratched at him.

Duggan's men edged forward, debating what they should do with silent glances until one man paced over to the fighting couple, aiming to drag her off. He slapped a hand on her shoulder, but only got an elbow in the guts for his trouble. The other men hooted with derision and, annoyed now, he paced around them, put his back to the edge and leaned down.

Although Mary didn't plan it, she and Duggan then happened to roll towards him, knocking into his ankles. Being off-balance he slipped. He put out a foot to keep himself upright, but that foot landed on air. He wheeled his arms, fighting for his balance but he was unable to arrest his backward motion and he tumbled over the side of the ledge.

This stopped the other men from

hooting and in a sudden understanding of the developing seriousness of the situation Duggan barked out a command for someone to help him get Mary off him. Both men moved for him, ignoring Jeff, who took this as his chance to act. He ran for the coil of rope, which Mary had brought up to the ledge earlier and dumped by the crane. He grabbed it, turned to the cage, and hurled an end towards the cage.

As the rope snaked out over the space Ethan risked releasing his grip from the side of the cage and grabbed the rope from the air. They had only seconds before the men separated Duggan and Mary, so Ethan had to risk moving quickly. As he paced into the open doorway, he decided to lasso the pulley and swing out to the ledge. He started to shout to Jeff that he should release the rope. But he was too late. Distressed timbers snapped on either side of him.

Then the base collapsed, the cage

effectively splitting in two, and all the debris was already too far away to grab. He fell. He still held the rope and a faint hope crossed his mind that Jeff might be able to brace himself sufficiently to keep hold of it and save him. He jerked his head up but couldn't see Jeff as he'd already fallen so far that the ledge was above him. The underside flashed into view. Then he was swinging towards the rock face beneath the ledge. An uncontrolled cry of alarm sounded and Ethan presumed he had made it.

He considered releasing the rope to avoid dragging Jeff with him, but the resolve that had kept him alive through the last few hours made him keep his grip. He swung towards the wall of rock, then jerked to a halt and swung backwards. He looked up, seeing that he'd come to rest dangling beneath the ledge. Somehow Jeff had arrested his fall, but Ethan didn't reckon he'd be able to support his weight for long. He had to climb and do it quickly.

He clawed hand over hand up the rope, his legs struggling to grab hold of the rope to aid his ascent. The climb was over twenty feet and the situation on the ledge had been so desperate he reckoned someone was sure to interfere with whatever Jeff had done to save him. So he threw all his efforts into climbing. He clambered up the length of the ledge and slapped a hand over the top, then raised his head above ground level.

The scene he faced was bad, but was better than he'd feared. Duggan had overcome Mary and was sitting on her chest working off his anger by slapping her face. One man was standing over them waiting for a chance to grab her if he needed to. Twenty feet to their side Jeff had succeeded in looping the rope around the struts of the crane and was taking the strain with a leg raised and braced against a strut. But Duggan's other man was standing over him and barking threats at him to release the rope.

The relieved Jeff smiled when he saw Ethan emerge but then tumbled forward when Duggan's man clubbed the back of his head. He hit the ground, releasing his grip of the rope. Ethan felt a sudden lurch, but he was already thrusting out his arms and he clung on to the ledge as the rope snaked away beneath him. His feet wheeled as he sought purchase on the rock until a foot caught and with a shove downwards he clawed himself up on to the rock to roll and lie flat.

He came to a halt looking towards Mary. Duggan had noticed his arrival and was gesturing to his companion to capture him. Ethan jumped to his feet, then looked at Jeff who was now lying on the ground. His assailant was dragging back a foot ready to kick him, but Jeff was ignoring his assailant and pointing. Ethan set off towards him thinking he was requesting help but then he saw what he was pointing at. The knife Mary had brought up earlier was lying beside the crane and towards the edge.

Ethan changed his movement and hurried towards it.

Duggan's man went for his gun. Seeing gunmetal flash to his side Ethan threw himself to the ground. A slug tore into the rock, winging past his legs as he dived over the knife. He gathered it up in his grasp, rolled again and came to a halt within the structure of the crane and looking back towards the man. The man fired but Ethan's luck held as the bullet tore into wood and ricocheted away.

Ethan braced himself then drew back his arm and hurled the knife. The man took aim again, but then panicked and tried to flinch away from the spinning knife. He was too late. The knife flew through the air, shining in the light from the low moon, and transfixed itself in his neck. He went down clawing at the hilt, but Ethan put him from his mind and turned to Jeff.

Jeff had now gathered heart from Ethan's success and the two men were struggling, but Jeff's assailant easily battered Jeff's arms aside, then grounded him with a sharp uppercut that sent him stumbling into the crane. The strut that had already been weakened when Jeff had used it to save Ethan creaked dangerously, then partly snapped, although it still held.

Ethan set off to help him, but he hadn't realized how close to the edge he was standing. His foot slipped, catching on the very edge. He fell forward and spent a frantic few moments clawing at the rock, ensuring he wouldn't tumble over the side. When he was sure he wouldn't fall he shook himself and started to rise only to find that Jeff's assailant had subdued Jeff and was standing over him.

The man kicked out, aiming to bundle him over the edge, but Ethan ducked beneath the foot then pushed off from the ground, grabbing the leg as he rose. The man landed flat on to his back, shook himself, and started to rise, but a firm kick to the chin flattened him again. Then Ethan jumped over him and turned. He looped a foot under his back and kicked upwards, bundling him over the edge.

And that just left Duggan.

He swirled round to find that he was already too late. Duggan had risen from Mary and had turned a gun on him. Jeff was sitting back against the crane with his hands thrust high. Mary was lying sprawled and possibly unconscious at Duggan's feet.

Ethan reckoned he had no hope. Nobody could help him. The only weapon that wasn't in Duggan's hands was with the dead man, and he was thirty feet away. The low moon cast the crane's long shadow across the ledge with Duggan standing at the apex, darkness wreathing his face. Slowly Duggan stepped forward out of the shadow to face Ethan.

'Was it worth it?' Jeff asked. 'Everything you did here and back in Bitter Creek was just to take over from Ansel, but you lost everything and everyone to get what you wanted. There's nothing left for you here.'

'Except Ansel's woman, and this stronghold, and . . . ' Duggan grunted, keeping his gaze on Ethan. 'I have everything. You have nothing but the lead you'll both get in the guts.'

'Come closer,' Jeff said.

'Why?' Duggan said, looking at Jeff for the first time.

'I have something to tell you. The one thing you never figured out.'

'You have nothing to say to me,' Duggan said.

Ethan knew Jeff was only talking to give them a chance to act, but during all the time he'd spent with him Jeff had been scared. Now Jeff sat with his back against the crane in a relaxed posture that showed more confidence than Ethan had ever seen him display.

Suddenly Ethan realized what Jeff planned to do. The moon was shining through the crane and into Duggan's eyes, and that meant he might suffer a moment of confusion when Jeff acted. Ethan vowed to buy Jeff that moment.

'He does,' Ethan said. 'The money

266

from the Bitter Creek bank raid isn't here, but we know where it is.'

Jeff flashed a brief smile as Ethan took the hint. Luckily this bait intrigued Duggan and he took a long pace towards him.

'Where?'

Ethan beckoned him on, judging that Duggan only needed to take another pace before Jeff could complete his plan. Duggan took that pace. Ethan smiled, then pointed beyond the edge, drawing Duggan's attention away.

Duggan glanced to the side and so didn't see Jeff brace his legs then thrust himself backwards against the crane strut, snapping it in two. With a huge grinding of timbers the crane toppled forwards.

Ethan leapt backwards to avoid the crane as it crashed down, as did Jeff, but Duggan moved too slowly. He snapped round to look at the crane, then jerked his head back, clearly unsure as to what was happening. Then he realized the danger he was in and threw an arm up before his face a moment before the crane hit him, pinning him to the ground.

The structure was still settling as Ethan jumped to his feet and hurried over to the man he'd killed earlier. He took his gun and ran over to the trapped Duggan, aiming to kill him, but Jeff shouted out.

'Don't!'

'Why not?' Ethan said, striding through the broken timbers to reach Duggan. He saw that Duggan's gun arm was trapped, other timbers lying on his legs and chest. He moved round so that he could see a bright ginger crop of hair, looking like the blood that would now flow. He aimed the gun down at him, letting the image of Sam Pringle fill his mind before he pulled the trigger.

'Duggan can clear your name. That is what you wanted, isn't it?'

Ethan looked at Duggan, the man he hated. Then he looked at Jeff, a man who had lied to him and got Sam

Pringle killed. Then he looked at Mary, a woman who he'd lied to but for whom he'd carried out Lansford's revenge when he'd killed Ansel Stark.

Ethan had to admit he had forgotten what it was he really wanted. His desperate battle to survive really had overcome his thoughts of revenge and clearing his name.

'I guess you're right,' he said, lowering his gun. 'I only ever wanted one thing — justice.'

12

'You picked a good position for him,' Mary said, standing before Lansford's grave.

Dawn was still some hours away and so in the darkness the surrounding terrain wasn't visible, but from what Ethan could remember of it, this was an elevated spot that could be seen for miles around.

'We did,' Ethan said cautiously.

'I don't know why you didn't tell me he was dead, but I can't worry about that now. Please just leave me with him.'

'I am sorry though. And I'm sorry if I shouldn't have done this, but I took something from him for you.'

Ethan held out the locket Lansford had been holding when he'd died. With a strangulated sob, Mary took it from him to clutch it to her chest.

'Thank you,' she whispered.

'It meant a lot to him.' Ethan turned to go, but she raised a hand, halting him.

'You spent time with him,' she said, her voice hoarse. 'How was he?'

Ethan shot a glance at Jeff, who winced, silently stating that he shouldn't lie to her again.

'He cared for you a lot, and you were the last thing on his mind when he died.'

'But how did he cope for two years while trying to find me?'

Ethan fought to find the right words to utter on this subject, but it was Jeff who answered.

'He was a good man,' he said. 'Brave and fearless and he stood by his friends. We both owe our lives to him and we both miss him.'

This politic comment satisfied Mary and she turned her back on them. She looped the locket around her neck then lowered her head over the grave.

Ethan and Jeff withdrew to a

respectful distance, standing a few yards from the Clancy sisters.

'I'm surprised you could bring yourself to say that,' Ethan said quietly while watching her, 'after everything you said to me about telling the truth.'

'I got you into a heap of trouble when I lied to you, and you made things worse when you lied to her.' Jeff sighed. 'But perhaps not all untruths have to be bad.'

Ethan considered his response carefully before he made it.

'They don't. Not when they're made for good reasons by decent people.'

'That mean you've accepted my apology?'

'I guess we both came out here to right a wrong. You'd caused some of that wrong, but your role wasn't as bad as Duggan's was and besides, Mary Donner, the Clancy daughters and myself are alive thanks to you. You've made amends for your actions, and that's all a man can ever do.'

Jeff sighed with relief and patted

Ethan's shoulder as he offered the nearest he could to forgiveness for his actions.

'And when we're finished here the truth is the only thing that'll clear your name. So when we return to Bitter Creek I'll tell everyone the full truth about Duggan Ward.'

'And you reckon that'll work, what with all Duggan's connections?'

'I do.' Jeff glanced at the Clancy sisters. 'And if anyone still doubts the truth, returning these two women safely should be enough to convince them that Duggan is an evil man.'

Duggan had broken an arm and a leg when the crane fell on him. The pain he was in, and would suffer on the return journey, as he lay on a hastily built travois was already providing its own form of retribution. By the time they reached Bitter Creek he would be in the right frame of mind to make a full confession.

'It should,' Ethan agreed. 'But that truth is sure to look bad for you. You could face a jail stretch for your role in the massacre.'

'And I deserve it.'

Ethan nodded. Then, feeling that he ought to do something else to make amends for his own actions, he headed over to join Mary. They both stood in silent tribute to another decent man who had suffered at the hands of Duggan Ward.

Presently she declared herself ready to leave and so, at a respectful pace, the small group headed out of the pass to set off on the journey back to Bitter Creek.

Ethan rode alone at the front, but when they reached the plateau he dropped back to join Jeff, who was keeping an eye on Duggan Ward. He considered Duggan's pained expression, his face pale and drawn as he was trundled over the rocky ground. He reckoned the injured man would give them no more trouble. He turned to Jeff.

'Come on,' he said, offering Jeff a

smile. 'There's no need for you to ride at the back with that man.'

Jeff returned the smile and the two men hurried to the front. Ahead, first light was reddening the horizon with the promise of a new day.

THE END

We do hope that you have enjoyed reading this large print book.

Did you know that all of our titles are available for purchase?

We publish a wide range of high quality large print books including:
Romances, Mysteries, Classics
General Fiction
Non Fiction and Westerns

Special interest titles available in large print are:
The Little Oxford Dictionary
Music Book, Song Book
Hymn Book, Service Book

Also available from us courtesy of Oxford University Press:
Young Readers' Dictionary
(large print edition)
Young Readers' Thesaurus
(large print edition)

For further information or a free brochure, please contact us at:
Ulverscroft Large Print Books Ltd.,
The Green, Bradgate Road, Anstey,
Leicester, LE7 7FU, England.
Tel: (00 44) **0116 236 4325**
Fax: (00 44) **0116 234 0205**

LIZARD WELLS

Caleb Rand

After losing his whole family to a bloodthirsty army patrol, Ben Brooke takes to the desolate Ozark snowline. Years later, he returns to the town called Lizard Wells, where the guilty soldiers have degenerated into guerrillas, bringing brutal disorder to the town. Also living there is the tough Erma Flagg — and more importantly, Moses, a young Cheyenne half-breed . . . After a wild thunderstorm crushes the town, Ben, in desperate need of help, chooses to step single-handedly into a final reckoning.

MISFIT LIL FIGHTS BACK

Chap O'Keefe

Misfit Lil wouldn't allow the rustlers to run off some of her pa's improved Flying G beeves. She started a stampede that trampled them bloodily into the dust. But then two assassins gunned down horse rancher Sundown Sander's son Jimmie. And he had made no move to defend himself, despite Lil's stormy ride to bring him warning. Could devious madam Kitty Malone or gambling-hall owner Flash Sam Whittaker tell the truth about Jimmie's fatal resignation? Lil had to find out.

SHOOT-OUT AT BIG KING

Lee Lejeune

Billy Bandro arrives in Freshwater Creek in Wyoming to start a new life away from riding with the killer outlaw Wesley Toms. When Toms is captured, Billy is assigned to drive him to Laramie for trial, but Toms' gang bushwhack the coach, leave Billy for dead, and take Nancy Partridge and her Aunt Emily hostage. The gambler Slam Beardsley saves Billy, and they ride off in pursuit. But there are many surprises for them in the mountains . . .

ROLLING THUNDER

Owen G. Irons

The town, once a thriving community, was now rotten. Even Tyler Holt, who'd never been browbeaten, lay dead, lynched by a mob. It was all down to Tom Quinn, leader of the first settlers, to return Stratton to its former prosperity. Stratton Valley, with its lush grass, rightfully belonged to him, but what could he do? As he faced the might of Peebles and his cohorts who controlled Stratton, only his courage and gun skills could save the day . . .

MASSACRE AT EMPIRE FASTNESS

P. McCormac

Butch Shilton and Joe Peters are both out of work when fate deals them a ten-year stretch in prison. But they soon find themselves the only survivors of the massacre at Empire Fastness Way Station and they set out to track down the killers. However, Butch and Joe are accused of the massacre, and, faced with a posse on their trail and the killers of Empire Fastness Way Station hunting them down, their chances of survival are slim . . .